A Lost Roma

Five more missions before forever begins...

Deb Laubach
Ray Caragher

Cover Design ©Christopher Hawke - CommunityAuthors.com

ISBN-13:978-0-9985290-1-1

Also available in A Twisted Series:
Twisted in Time – Book One

Coming next in A Twisted Series:
A Twisted Reality – Book Three
The Curse of Love – Book Four

Acknowledgments

We cannot thank The Powers That Be, the Cosmic Tumblers, Open-Mindedness and Awareness enough.

We thank our spouses and our children for *understanding who we really are* and believing in our dream. Thank you for loving and supporting us, while accepting each time we said, "Just one more chapter," knowing that it would turn into countless more hours and one less plate to set at dinnertime. We love you.

Endless thank yous to our visionary team of experts at CommunityAuthors.com: Traci Hall and Christopher Hawke for their tireless assistance.

May we all be filled with Love: Consideration, Compassion, and Compromise. Love is timeless and always reveals Herself and She knows no boundaries - for She is Love.

Chapter 1

August 10, 1944 - 6:30 p.m.

"Only five more missions to go," Tommy Smith said aloud. By luck or some kind of magical spell, he'd just completed his twentieth flight. And as if by divine intervention, he now had been given an unexpected three-day leave while repairs were done on his plane's fuselage, that had been damaged during a German fighter attack.

The young American B-17 pilot raced against the fading sunlight in an attempt to reach his destination before the blackout ordinance went into effect. He decided to leave the base right after debriefing, skipping his usual shower to not waste a single moment, he needed to be with *her*.

The quaint English village of Royston was only three miles from Bassingbourn Royal Air Force Base. The rolling farmland, dotted with islands of trees, filled the late evening air with the scent of freshly cut hay as he made his way down the wet, uneven cobblestone street. Normally, this would have made him feel like he was home in Wisconsin. But on this mid-August night, his mind was not back home; instead, it was spiraling out of control into a dark hole.

Tommy neared Christie's Crown Pub when he suddenly couldn't get the slow-motion image of the China Breeze, the lead plane in today's mission, out of his head as it lost its wing from anti-aircraft fire. Helpless, he'd watched with horror as it exploded. No visible survivors parachuted out of the plane. His breaths shortened, his chest ached. The realization of what he'd experienced a few hours before was finally hitting him. Hard. He'd barely landed his own damaged plane.

His hands shook and he gasped for air as he recalled *Fifinella*, his B-17, shudder from the attack. There were cries from the crew as he and Louis, his co-pilot, checked the gauges while holding the plane on course. They could smell the high-octane fuel that leaked across the wing as they waited for the explosion that never came. *No wonder I'm a mess.*

He leaned against the closest brick building in an attempt to catch his breath, clutching at his chest while bending over, trying not to regurgitate his preflight meal.

I can't let her see me like this. She already worries every time I leave as it is... but today... Jesus Christ! Air! I need air! Get your shit together man! Rachel. Rachel Christie Smythe. Breathe. He repeated her name silently over and over in his head. *Just breathe. Don't let her see you fall apart. At all. Ever. Breathe, damn it!*

His thoughts were interrupted by Ray, a fellow pilot, who shouted from a pub across the street, "Tommy, you okay?"

Tommy quickly straightened up attempting to hide his jitters. "Yeah, yeah. Just something I ate. I'll be fine." He waved his friend off and Ray went back into the pub, allowing laughter to be heard for the mere seconds the door was open.

He began to regain his bearings as he pictured Rachel's beautiful face and eyes smiling at him. Finally, after a few more minutes, Tommy's anxiety receded and he started for the Crown. He just needed her to hold him; she was always his brightest star on the darkest night.

The coolness of the evening air filled his lungs. The sound of children laughing as mothers called them home to dinner rang in his ears. A couple of kids with a soccer ball in hand ran past him on their way—he dodged to his left as two people rode up behind him ringing their bicycle bells in friendly warning. The small street closed down for the night. He allowed himself to enjoy the beautiful sunset visible between the roofs of the brick and stone buildings that led to Rachel.

Tommy walked the remaining blocks, arriving at his destination. He pulled the old wooden door of Christie's Crown Pub back and slipped past the blackout curtain. He stood just inside, letting the aroma of food and cigarettes fill his head. The family pub was hopping with people while the sounds of laughter, friendly arguments, and talk filled his ears. There were cracks of the billiard balls, along with heated discussions over a game of darts and the like that were so familiar and soothing.

For a moment, there was no world war going on.

He sat down on a stool along the old wooden bar while studying the mirrored back wall that had glass shelves lined with all kinds of liquor. He was barely acclimated to his surroundings when he saw Rachel out of the corner of his eye running toward him. He stood up to embrace her as her arms and legs wrapped around him, pulling her body tightly against his. "Oh, my sweet Tommy!" She nuzzled her face into his neck and gently planted kisses on him.

He'd only been gone for three days, but it felt like three years had passed since he had last held her. The intoxicating scent of her hair and skin filled his brain replacing the foul smell of aviation fuel.

"Baby, I missed you so much! I didn't expect to see you for a couple more days," she whispered. Tears filled her emerald green eyes, while the rims of her irises turned a deeper and more distinct blue than usual—almost as if her eyes were green *and* blue.

Before he could respond she kissed him, sliding her tongue between his lips. She brought his senses back to life as the taste of her mouth lingered in his. She sat him back on his stool. "Tommy, I'll get you an ale. I have a few orders to bring over to some tables. I love you."

"Thanks, beautiful." He was glad he didn't need to tell her why he was back so soon. He watched as her petite, slender, perfectly proportionate body swayed away. Her long chestnut-brown hair tied up in a ponytail bounced back and forth between her shoulders.

He sat at the long, burled wood bar waiting for his ale when he felt his 5' 10" athletic body begin to tremble. *"Damn it!"* He muttered to himself while squeezing his eyes shut and pulling his hands through his thick dark hair, hoping when he opened his eyes that he would be in Baraboo, Wisconsin. He opened his eyes. *Fuck! Instead I'm in an English pub because of the Second World War. But fuck! Fuck! Then Rachel wouldn't be in my life.*

Rachel, on the other side of the bar, held a pint of dark ale in a frosty mug. "Tommy, you're home now, sweetheart."

The worried look in her eyes caused him to instantly respond. "Just a rough mission, Rach, so sorry. I don't want you to worry. On a good note, I have been given leave for the next three nights." Tommy took a big slug of beer attempting to snap himself back into the here and now. "So, my love, what's for dinner tonight?"

He watched her expression morph into teasing mode, and he guessed it would be something with Spam. "Well, Lieutenant," she attempted not to smile, "Tonight we have two entrees: creamed Spam on a biscuit or Spam stew. Which would you prefer?" Her arms crossed as she waited for him to answer.

"Well, Miss, they both sound so good... hmm, what do I want to order?"

"Maybe something you've had before, Lieutenant?" Rachel had a sassy sparkle in her eyes as she leaned forward on her elbows and rested her chin on her folded hands.

He grinned. "How about another beer—with a kiss."

"Well, my, my." Straightening, she put her hands on her hips. "I'm sorry to see that your high-altitude sickness hasn't gotten any better since the day we met." Rachel turned and walked back to the kitchen. He found himself staring at her pear-shaped ass as it gently rocked back and forth and disappeared into the kitchen.

He was trying desperately to push away the visions from earlier in the day, that his brain vividly ran *over* and *over,* when he heard a couple sitting at a table close by talking about going on a short holiday—camping somewhere in the outskirts of England. Sipping the rest of his ale, his mind drifted back to a camping trip along Devil's Lake in Wisconsin with his younger brother, Robert.

Tommy's recollections were interrupted by the frosty mug placed in front of him. He looked up to find Rachel's face only inches away as she leaned over the bar.

"Your order is here." She slid it onto the counter. "Unfortunately, we have run out of Spam—but I was lucky enough to secure you the last order of Shepherd's pie and a slice of apple pie, too. I hope you don't mind."

She pulled his face to hers and gave him a long, passionate kiss. "Don't make a big deal about the frosty mug, I only do it for you. I'm off in forty-five minutes, Lieutenant. You want to walk me home?"

"Well, yes ma'am. If you feel safer with a soldier, I would be happy to escort you home.

Rachel stood with her hands on her hips and fire in her heart. *This war doesn't need a bomb or a death to destroy you.*

"God, Rachel do I ever need you tonight…" Moisture pooled in Tommy's cobalt blue eyes and his hands shook as he picked up his mug. Rachel knew something bad must have happened and tried to comfort him. "Tommy…" she came around the bar and wrapped her arms around his neck. "Sweetheart, I'm here for you."

"Where's Izzy tonight?"

"She's home. Seems it was her turn to be the welcoming committee. Lucky harlot!"

"Rachel!" Ian's voice boomed from the kitchen as the cook shouted, "Order up!"

"I have to…"

Tommy cut her off. "I know—go, babe."

She walked quickly to the kitchen to retrieve her order the whole time thinking about Tommy—wanting to know what had happened. Suddenly it occurred to her that maybe Alex had been wounded. *Oh my God… Izzy must be going crazy!*

Izzy was Rachel's best friend since childhood and Alex was Tommy's navigator and *his* best friend. Izzy and Alex had clicked immediately the night Tommy brought Alex to the pub after having spent his leave with Rachel back in May. Here it was mid-August and the two couples were madly in love.

The next forty-five minutes seemed endless as she waited on customers and quickly cleaned up her station. She arranged for another waitress to cover her shifts for the next three days so she could spend every minute with Tommy while he was on leave.

Toward the end of her shift, she brought him coffee and dessert. "Darling, here's your apple pie with some vanilla ice cream." She could tell that the sound of her voice startled him.

It seemed he was somewhere else. She had watched him staring into the mirror but not at his reflection. She knew he had visions like she did of things locked in the depth of their souls. It wasn't just the physical attraction that had brought them together—that was a bonus—but tonight his aura was different. She felt he was sad and frightened though he came back to the present.

He smiled. "Wow, that looks good, babe. You made it?"

"Yes, Lieutenant, baking gives me something to do when you're away to keep me out of trouble with other soldiers. As they say, idle hands are the work of the devil…" She kissed his cheek.

"Then give me those hands, they're mine." He repeatedly kissed her hands while she giggled at him.

The hurried pace of the pub slowed as patrons thinned out. She asked timidly, "Tommy, is Alex okay?"

"Yeah, he's fine. I know he was heading to Izzy's tonight. Why?"

"No reason." She walked away to clean up while Tommy finished his coffee.

She had inherited the pub when her parents were killed in a bombing raid in London. The patrons loved her for the way she took care of them, making each one of them feel important.

At last the pub was empty but for the staff when Rachel spoke in a stern voice, "Sir, we are closing. You will need to leave now." Her body teemed with excitement.

"But I never received my bill, Miss."

"It's your lucky night—the owner of the establishment has decided to pick up the tab for you since you are suffering from high-altitude sickness and in need of a long warm bath with a hot-to-trot woman." She stood in front of him with her sweater over her shoulder and a huge smile on her face.

"Wow! That is *really* great. I know where there's a nice tub. Any idea on the hot-to-trot woman?" He looked squarely into her face and grinned from ear-to-ear.

"Oh, I see. In that case, dinner is a hundred pounds and Ethel's in back. See you the next time you have leave, you bugger!"

Tommy laughed as he embraced her, sharing a long, deep passionate kiss. "Let's go, baby."

He helped her put her sweater on and they walked outside into the cool night air. The light from a million stars illuminated the way down the cobblestone street as they began their short journey to her cottage. He slipped his arm around her waist. Rachel followed suit, pulling them tightly together, both knowing each step they took brought them closer to what they desperately wanted—lovemaking and a lifetime with each other.

Chapter 2

Rachel hoped the cool of the evening air along with the closeness of their bodies would open Tommy up to let her back into his world. How to lift the heaviness she felt around them? Letting go of him, she stopped walking and pointed toward the sky. "Tommy, look at the sliver of the moon. It's smiling at us. See?"

He stared directly into her face, visually tracing her arm to the tip of her pointing finger. He finally looked up at the moon.

"Baby, it is smiling at us, isn't it? I'll try to shake off this bad feeling." Before he could say more, she leaned into him, and planted a sweet, lingering kiss on his lips. Their kiss ended with a meaningful smile but it didn't break the unusual spell that filled the air. Continuing down the street she decided not to pry any further, understanding that he needed time to work through whatever was going on in his head.

She opened the gate that led down the curvy path to the door of the white bungalow with a thatched roof. Tommy hesitated about halfway on the path as if caught by the scent of hollyhocks and lavender. Rachel stood by the entrance. "Come on, Tommy."

"My God, isn't the garden we planted beautiful, Rachel?" He inhaled deeply. The flowers that lined both sides of the path were almost at his chest height. In the late twilight, the brilliant colors were still visible. The ground had become blanketed with their petals. "This is how royalty must feel."

"Come on! You silly bugger, we'll play in the garden in the morning." Smiling, she returned to him and grabbed his arm, pulling him toward the opened door.

Rachel felt uneasy as she watched him just stand there like it was the first time, or perhaps, the *last* time he would see it. "What's going on with you my fly-boy? I feel there is something that you are keeping to yourself. Before you reply, I just want you to remember our love is eternal. What are you thinking about, Tommy? Where are you, my love?"

"I'm home." He answered with a sheepish grin on his face.

"Perfect." *God he's killing me.* "Have a whiskey then, and you know better than to ask for ice." She tried again to lift his spirits.

Tommy came out of his fog for a moment and laughed. "You always tease."

"Think you could make me a fire tonight without burning our house down, fly-boy?"

"Hey, I now know where the hose is if I need it." He smiled at her. She was glad to see that he was perhaps coming out of his funk.

"Sure it's safe for me to take a quick bath?" She leaned against the wall, unbuttoning her blouse.

"You're in good hands, my lady. I am available to scrub your back if you like." He started to unbutton his shirt.

"Humph. Thank you, Lieutenant, but I will be quick. Don't forget to open the damper." She watched as he poured himself a whiskey.

"Pardon me, princess." He lifted his tumbler in a sarcastic salute. "Enjoy your bath. You remind me of a drill sergeant I knew back in the States."

Rachel giggled as she walked into the bedroom, hoping the sparks she just saw in him would bring him back from the razor's edge he balanced on.

While she bathed, her thoughts were wildly consumed with Tommy's strange behavior. Although he was attentive and loving, something was just off and she knew in her heart that he wasn't telling her the whole story. *Just a rough one,* she thought. *It must have been a* really *rough one. Five more missions and then I have him forever.*

⋯⇒◉⇐⋯

Tommy sipped his whiskey, surrounded by the warmth of who Rachel was—the photos, the homey décor, the high-beamed ceilings, a large stone fireplace. *What an amazing woman. I hope we can live happily ever after when this is over. I don't want to ever lose her. I've finally found my other half, my equal. Thank you. I guess my prayers were heard. It only took a world war for me to find the love of my life.*

He felt at home as he walked across the room, and the wooden floors creaked under the weight of his body. He grinned when opening the flue, watching the kindling smolder beneath the logs. After another drink, he sat down in front of the fireplace watching the flames. Hearing the tub fill with water, knowing Rachel was naked in the next room excited him; he wished this moment would never end, until the dark side of his thoughts loomed…

Hell, I could be dead in a week. She's already been through so much. She lost her fiancé, parents and God knows who else to this fucking war. Why fuck her life up anymore because of me?

He recalled Rachel's best friend Izzy warning him the night he decided to ask Rachel out: "Don't break her heart." *God, that seems so long ago but it's only been a few months. Time is irrelevant. I cling to each second as if it's my last. Watching people die or live is such a random act with no reason attached to the why. In the middle of all this craziness I have found the most important thing: The one I want to spend the rest of my life with.*

Pouring his third whiskey, he tried to relax while listening to the crackle and pop of the wood burning. But his mind churned. *Why would anybody want to be in love with a fucking soldier? What a waste!* He thought of the young waste gunner who was badly wounded earlier that day. *And to think he pinch hit for Rich who was sick. It could have been Rich on his twentieth mission.*

When Rachel returned she was wearing a robe with a towel wrapped around her hair. "Hey, fly-boy, what does it take for a lady to get a drink around here?"

"Stay just the way you are." He admired her body as he poured her a drink. "Here you go, Miss. Sorry, we're out of ice."

"Thank God," she muttered. "You know I prefer my whiskey neat."

He handed her the drink and noticed that her hands were trembling. He sat down next to her on the loveseat. "Rachel, I haven't been able to get you out of my mind since the day we first met, you know."

Bloody hell, this sounds serious. She sat, apprehensive. Tommy grabbed his drink and took a deep swallow.

Before he could speak she said, "Tommy, *I am in love with you!* Since the moment our eyes met, I knew. Our first kiss only confirmed what my mind already knew, what my heart and soul were screaming at me…"

He smiled a sad smile in response and looked down at his glass. Rachel studied him. "What's going on with you, my love? You're not ending this with me, are you?"

She stared at him waiting nervously for his reply, which didn't come. The only sound she heard was his deep breathing and almost what she thought was his heart beating–or hers–thumping in her ears.

"Tommy, is this what's going on with you tonight? You want out?"

Tommy looked at her. "No! No! Not at all!" He pulled her into his arms and kissed her deeply. "Rachel, you are my love, my heart, my home. You own my heart. The rest of it doesn't matter."

"Darling, you're all over the place tonight, and the rest of it does matter. You are only here physically. The rest of you is someplace else so far away. If I'm yours and this is your home, then hold my hand." She held his hand tightly. "Come home, my love, for I am right here." Tears rolled down her cheeks.

"I'm so fucked up." He squeezed her hand. "We were attacked by a German fighter today. It could have been fatal had the fuel leaking from the wing exploded."

"Oh my God! Was any of the crew hurt?"

Tommy rubbed his throat and nodded.

They sat in silence on the loveseat intertwined, almost like one body. She heard the drops of rain begin to hit the roof... Rachel rolled onto his lap and leaned her entire body against his as their desire for each other burned like wildfire. She relished the softness of his lips as they kissed and the taste of his mouth as their tongues desperately danced.

She felt the stiffness growing between his legs, and realized her mouth was watering with desire to lick, suck, taste, tease, and be one with him. She pulled him up from the loveseat and he could barely control his passion as they made their way toward the bedroom. She guided him to the bathroom, where she filled the tub for him.

"I want to make love to you, not the bloody airplane aftershave you're wearing." She sat on the floor next to the tub. "I won't leave your side my love…" She held his hand as he lay back into the cleansing, warm soapy water.

❧⟖◉⟗❧

Back in the bedroom, he pulled her into him from behind with his hard erection resting against her bare ass. He was sexually and mentally charged for her–only her.

"Tommy!" She turned to face him. "Baby, slow down, I'm all yours…I'm your lover, not a mission you're on. You're home, darling."

"Sorry, Rach, you have cast another spell on me." He pulled her gently against his body.

"My sweet Tommy, I love you. And need you."

Everything disappeared in the world except the need to be lost in each other. She pushed him back onto the bed and climbed on top of him.

"Tommy, I *need* you!"

"I love you, Rachel."

She straddled his naked body, his cock against her slippery lips between her legs. It slid easily into her as she was already sopping wet. She let out a moan of pleasure as he began to fill her with his steely length.

Their grinding and thrusting became immediately in sync, melding into one singular motion when she quickly cried out, "Yes, my sweet Tommy!" He could feel her beginning to climax with each grind of her hips, her expression morphing into a lioness ready to devour her prey. Tommy pulled her ass into him, so he could bury himself as deeply into her as possible while listening to Rachel's moans and indecipherable words.

His body gave into the sensuous walls of her pussy as it clamped around his cock.

For a moment time stood still.

Looking into each other's eyes, they were one–totally lost in space–time did not exist–just the purest pleasure of their naked flesh and souls completely bared to the other. They simultaneously exploded into ecstasy sharing the most intimate and sensual orgasm either had ever experienced.

"Rachel!" Tommy managed to say while his eyes focused on her beautiful face, as he filled her with his passionate climax.

What they shared was beyond making love. Rachel and Tommy combined both facets of the God-given gift of being a man and woman along with the intertwining of their souls.

Chapter 3

August 11, 1944 – 2:30 a.m.

Tommy woke a few hours later, listening to Rachel softly breathe as she slept next to him. He slipped out of bed and gently closed the door to the bedroom. He poured himself a whiskey and saw the wood still aglow in the fireplace. He added a log to the smoldering embers.

Wishing his dream hadn't woken him, he sat on the bay window seat and sipped his whiskey, hoping it would quiet his mind and bring about more sleep.

In his dream, he'd been a young child. They were all sitting around a campfire and he was listening to two men talking in a language foreign to him, yet he understood every word. He drank hot liquid from a mug as they spoke about the meaning of life.

The man he felt was his father, but who wasn't Tommy's dad, told the story to the other man whose name was Uncle Hendrik about how their father had left Europe with his wife, Becka and their sister, Gretuda. The man he thought was his dad then looked at him. "Boy, your Grandfather Roelf came here with nothing but the clothes on his back and a dream for a different life for his family. When he left, he said good-bye to all his family and friends because he knew he would never return to see any of them again. You sometimes need to do the right thing because life is not only about you."

His dream continued with the elders talking late into the night and he, the child, fell asleep. It was the first glimmer of the sun as it peeked above the eastern edge of the sky that woke him. The air was cool and calm outside, the smells of the dampness from the black soil and the woods scented the air. Mourning doves called off in the distance, filling the air with their sweet cooing while the trees gently swayed in the morning breeze. The men were gone. He was all alone in the woods and no longer a child, but a man himself.

He sat up when suddenly a hand touched his shoulder from behind. Turning his head, their eyes met. "Tommy, I wanted to say good-bye while there is still time in this life."

It was his younger brother Robert.

"But, Rob, I'm not gone!"

Robert leaned forward and kissed his brow. It was that kiss that woke him. Reliving the dream, he touched his forehead. Was it moist from the kiss?

Leaning back against the window with a sigh, he picked up his glass and drained the remaining whiskey. He walked over to the decanter and poured himself another, then returned to his seat. He watched the fire while mulling over what the dream meant when he saw Rachel's stack of journals. She kept the latest one inside an old cigar box. Rachel was always jotting things down about their relationship, as well as dreams and thoughts she had, including her thoughts about past lives.

Tommy had questioned Rachel's sanity at first when she'd explained to him her theory about life. Over time, her words caused him to reconsider the many different things he always thought were just inexplicable coincidences in his life.

Opening the journal, a smile came to his face as he read an entry about the day they planted new bulbs of colorful flowers. He laughed when he recalled how he had to follow each of Rachel's orders to the enth degree on how to mix the soil. She was convinced it was her secret ingredients that she added to the soil which made the blooms so full of life with such rich colors…it consisted of all kinds of things that this farm boy had never heard of before.

He is teasing me and made fun of the "magical potion" that I needed to be mixed "just right" for my plants to grow perfectly… I love how he is watching me in my old overalls busily planting bulbs while getting covered in mud. The aroma of the wet soil he tells me reminds him of his days working on the farm in Wisconsin. He chuckled at how dirty and sweaty I'd become, hair amuck, face all smudged. Yet he said it still can't hide my natural beauty and how it radiated from within me. I'm always his brightest star on the darkest night.

She wrote down everything someone said to her, exactly. How many times would he find, "I love you Rachel Christie Smythe!"?

Closing the book, he set it down next to her neat stack of a dozen or more journals. He pulled out the bottom one which was marked 1932-33 on the cover.

He'd never looked at the first one. Opening it, the entry was dated, August 5th, 1932.

I have decided to record my life's events for those who want to know me. Myself included. My simple life is filled with dreams and thoughts about who I am, who I want to be, how I see the world. Enjoy my story…

Last night I went to a carnival. My parents allowed me to bring my friend Izzy with me. We walked the midway where all kinds of sideshows were going on. My parents decided to go on the Ferris wheel and gave us money to use as we pleased.

Me and Izzy were approached by a gentleman who offered to uncover our past lives. "Ladies, don't you want to know if maybe you were Cleopatra in your last life, or a princess? For a mere pound the past can be unlocked."

Izzy looked at me and grinned. She is the wild one but I love her so. She dared me to do it. "Izzy, I double dare you to do it!"

"Ladies, don't be afraid," the man in the bowler hat said to us. "What harm could it cause? Perhaps a mystery can be answered for you. In fact, it is your lucky night already, both of you can be regressed for only a pound instead of two. Maybe you will discover why you are best friends."

We finally agreed to do it if we went together. I was slightly hesitant as we walked down a narrow, tented corridor that opened up into a larger tented area. There, a rather frail gray-haired gentleman was seated on a chair in a dimly lit area with a couch that we were meant to lay upon during a reading, and another chair.

"Good evening ladies, my name is Dr. Cavanagh. Who wants to go first?"

Izzy suddenly became nervous and sat on the chair leaving me to lay down on the soft, velvety couch.

"What is your name, Miss?" He spoke in such a soft voice that I could barely hear him due to all the noises outside the tent.

I replied a bit louder. "Rachel."

"Rachel, please close your eyes. Clear your mind for we are no longer here in the tent. There is a beautiful garden filled with flowers and sunlight for you to explore. Do you smell them?"

"Yes. Yes, I do, Doctor. There are so many colors."

"Good. Now look for a path with stepping stones. Do you see it?"

"Yes. There's an enormous tree where the path begins."

"Rachel, the tree represents your soul's journey. Now let's start down the path." I walked down this path for a while until I reached the end. He said at the same time, "Stop. Look to your right. What do you see?"

"I am holding a baby. I am nursing her and she is looking into my eyes. But he is leaving me and taking our eldest son with him. It will be my son's first hunt. It's a large hunt for all of us. All of the hunters are going. He kisses our baby and then touches my face. He doesn't speak to me. We communicate through the look in our eyes."

Tommy was startled by Rachel's sleepy voice. "What are you doing, my love?" She sat down next to him, tying her robe.

"I was reading one of your journals. I hope you don't mind. You've only shown me the journal from the time we met. I never realized how far back your writing goes. God, I love you so much, Rachel Christie Smythe."

She put her arms around his neck pulling his lips into hers.

"I was also remembering how relentlessly you teased me when we planted the garden. 'Tommy! Thomas! Thomas Smith! Can you please pay closer attention to what you're doing? Our garden would grow better if you did!'" He laughed out loud.

"Which journal were you reading, love?" She stared at him while skipping over his last comment.

"The beginning. You and Izzy at the carnival. Do you think you know who it was that you described that night?"

"Yes! In fact, I'm certain it was you from a past life. I've been awaiting your arrival ever since that night. There is much more for you to read. But right now, and more importantly, is the fact that you are here and we are together."

A lump formed in his throat as he accepted the fact that she was referring to the reality of time and the chance he wouldn't return from a mission.

"Tommy, come and lay with me. I want your body next to mine."

Chapter 4

They were spooning on the bed under the feather comforter, shades drawn and the only light a candle on the dresser. Rachel finally broke the easy silence by inquiring, "You're coming up on your twenty-first mission, right?

"I am. Why do you ask, my love?"

Rachel hesitated as she weighed out what she was about to ask him. "Tommy, what did you think about the carnival entry?"

Tommy laughed softly. "The night when you and Izzy got talked into discovering your past lives?" His response was tainted with light sarcasm.

A Lost Romance Found

She rolled over so she could look into his face.

"Are you saying you don't think what I learned that night was anything important? You realize that I believe it pertains to us."

"Well, I'm not sure what I think about it all. It was a sideshow at a carnival, Rach. I'm not trying to put you down or anything. I guess I always thought of it as just entertainment, you know?"

He leaned forward and attempted to kiss her, but she turned her head while she tried to free herself from his embrace.

"Thomas Smith!" Rachel pushed him away. "Haven't you ever wondered why we were so drawn to each other immediately? Do you think I've hooked up with a countless string of blokes that showed up at my parents' pub like some bloody harlot?"

"No, because you were looking for a gardener with limited mental capacity and great muscles…" He laughed while looking into her eyes.

His reply enraged Rachel.

"I already told you I was waiting for you to show up, Mr. Smartass!" She spoke very sternly.

He realized she wasn't joking and sat up, resting his head on his knees. "You're serious, aren't you?"

She also sat up. "I bloody well am! You own me, Tommy. This is no joke to me." Her voice hitched.

Tommy gently stroked her soft cheek with his fingertips. "Sorry love, I didn't mean to be a shitty boyfriend. For the record, you know I was overcome by you the minute we met."

She sighed. "Go on." A slight smile hovered around her mouth.

"I'll never forget the first night we met. From that moment on, I couldn't get you out of my mind. Yes, it was a physical attraction at first, but the next few days and even during the next mission, all I thought about was your eyes. I was afraid you wouldn't go out with me and I was laughing at myself that a bomber pilot would worry about a barmaid saying no to him."

She straightened up and responded with slight defiance in her voice, "I'll ignore that last comment about barmaids and ask you this: do you believe we've been together before?"

Nothing was said between them for a few moments. They laid back down and watched the candlelight dance on the ceiling.

Tommy finally said, "I do *know* you. Something inside you has awoken me to this type of love… it's so natural and beautiful. But even more than that, I feel like I've known you since the beginning of time… and it overwhelms me. But how? I grew up in Wisconsin and you in England. So how do you figure all this?"

She rolled onto his chest and propped her chin on her hands while looking into his beautiful blue eyes. "In our past lives, my love. We've been reunited by powers greater than us."

He smiled. "Well, I have been searching for you for a long time. The night we met my brain screamed so loud I was afraid the whole pub would hear it." He laughed at himself.

"And I have watched your mind go off to places. Where is it that you go my beautiful fly-boy?"

He looked at her for a minute or two before answering. "God, you're beautiful."

"Tommy! I'm serious!" She frowned with tears in her eyes.

"Okay, okay," he said softly. "I have visions. I've been afraid of them my whole life. Sometimes I know things before they happen. I started thinking I was nuts, so I kept them to myself. At times, I chose to ignore the visions when I shouldn't have. I'm still learning."

"All the while I was waiting for you. Call it fate or destiny, it doesn't matter. We, my fly-boy, have been searching for each other, don't you see? Don't you feel it?"

It was as if he needed a few minutes to digest her words. "That makes some sense. And honestly, I'm not sure why I went to your particular pub the night we met. I passed by two other places but when I stood outside the Crown, I just felt a pull, and knew I had to go inside. It was like a calling. Who knows why, maybe because one of the mess hall cooks, Bill from Brooklyn, mentioned it to someone ahead of me in line. I don't recall anything he said about the place but something brought me there. Rach, I was just hungry and craving a room temperature beer, and I *found* you."

Rachel listened to him and smiled while snuggling into him. "So I'm not just a barmaid you met?"

"No, love. You're the other half of my heart, the tears of joy that fill my eyes. The softest and sweetest lips I have ever tasted. You are my reason to survive. I don't know what I would do without you."

Tommy, who had always been as solid as a rock, began to feel his emotions take over. He started to tremble and hoped she wasn't frightened by it.

She whispered, "My sweet love, you do understand that I want all of you? We aren't two fucked up, scared people clinging to each other just to make it through the craziness of a world war. I know we've been brought together for reasons beyond that, if only to show the world the depth of true love."

He looked at her realizing that for the first time in his life he truly had fallen in love.

"Would you go with me to see Doc Cavanagh?"

He lay back on the pillow. "I will, Rachel, if that's what you truly want. But what if we hear something we don't want to know? Like an unwanted truth about the future?"

She kissed his cheek. "I think we need to open the door to our future to figure out a way to stay connected to each other forever this time. We can't lose each other again, Tommy." She began to cry.

"Sweetheart, we won't ever be apart again. Only five more missions and I'm done. I love you so much! I wish I had another word for "love" to express the depth of what I feel for you." He wrapped his arms around her, pulling her against his body, and his desire for her began to rise.

"Always and all ways, right?" Rachel whispered, kissing him.

"Forever and ever," he whispered back as he lifted her up and pulled her on top of him, so he could look into her eyes.

She leaned down and began to suck on his bottom lip. She positioned her wet lips against his large, velvety length and he easily slid inside of her. Rachel's body responded immediately and she sat back so he could penetrate her as deeply as possible. She gasped with sheer pleasure as her wet pussy took every inch of him.

"Always and forever, Rach." His breath hitched with each word.

Within a short time of them slowly grinding with him deeply inside her, she climbed toward a climax. She attempted to focus on his eyes, and began to ride him feverishly and desperately.

Tommy couldn't hold back any longer and when she cried out, "My sweet Tommy, yes! Oh, baby! Yes! I'm coming... so... good..." her voice trailed off, replaced with moans of pleasure. Tears streamed down her face and she fell onto his chest as they looked into each other's eyes, sharing an explosive orgasm.

He began to softly cry as she sobbed with pleasure. She whispered, "I love you... I love you..."

"Rachel Smythe, I love you..."

They collapsed together with him still fitting perfectly inside her. Their breathing slowly returned to normal, and they drifted off to sleep.

‹—◉◉—›

Tommy woke up a few hours later and watched Rachel sitting on the edge of bed while thumbing through her journal.

"Baby, what are you doing?" he asked softly while she read an entry.

"My fly-boy, you can say no to what I'm about to ask."

"Well ask first and then I can say yes or no."

She put the tattered old journal down and laid her head on his chest.

"Rachel, what is it?"

"I *really* want you to meet the man from the carnival and let him open the door for us, regardless of what we may discover."

He closed his eyes and considered this in silence. *Everything about us is perfect except for the war.* He felt the softness of her hair and the taste of her body still lingered on his lips.

"Tommy, are you asleep?"

"No. But for a moment all I want is everything to stay just the way it is. No worries about life. However, if you think seeing this guy will open something that will make this last forever and ever, I'm in."

Rachel kissed him deeply. He smiled and fell back into a blissful sleep.

Chapter 5

Tommy woke up Friday morning, his official first full day of leave. He heard Rachel's voice in the other room and assumed she was on the telephone since there were no other voices in the cottage. But the warmth and softness of the covers caused him to drift back into a deep sleep.

He dreamt of living in a seaport where large ships were docked in the harbor outside his open bedroom window. Looking in the mirror he saw he was a man in his mid-thirties with dark hair and a well-trimmed beard, and he was getting ready to go to the shipyard. The room he was in was from a long time ago, but he was not caught up in his thoughts about his job. He only had thoughts of a woman with dark hair and porcelain skin that he loved. He was planning to end his career after this next cruise wanting to spend his life with her.

Suddenly he was jarred from the dream. "Come on, sleepyhead, I only have you for the next two and a half days." Rachel lay upon his chest in her purple silk day robe, and stared into his eyes with a "cat who ate the canary" expression.

Tommy grabbed her and rolled on top of her. "And what's wrong with just spending it right here in this nice bed?" He pinned her down with a huge smile on his face.

She tickled his waist. "God help me! Why did I fall in love with a fly-boy? Crikey! All they want is sex!"

The next few minutes were spent tickling each other which turned into passionate kissing. Suddenly she pushed him away and hopped out of bed, leaving the bedroom.

"Let's have breakfast!" she shouted from the other room. "I made you coffee and a nice crumb cake. And just for your gourmet pleasure, fresh squeezed orange juice."

He stayed in bed for a moment longer looking through the opened window. The sky was crystal blue, the birds were singing. *How lucky am I? Wasn't it just yesterday that I was being shot at and now this bliss? If I'm really lucky, it will last for the rest of my life.*

"Tommy, come on, the cake just came out of the oven!"

"Coming, my love." In his underwear, he entered the kitchen which was filled with the aroma of coffee and cinnamon. He sat down at the small wooden table in the breakfast nook and looked through the window at the glorious morning sky and their garden.

Tommy devoured the sweet crumb cake as Rachel told him about the plans that she'd made for the day: "First, we'll have lunch with my Aunt Marilyn, she's desperate to meet you, and then we'll go see Doc Cavanagh. Does that sound okay?"

He loved watching her lips as she spoke, so much that he barely registered what she was saying.

"Tommy?"

"Sure, sure. As long as we're together, I don't care what we do or where we go. As you said, we only have two and a half days."

"And as much as I would love to spend the whole time in bed," she said, "I'm on a mission of my own to uncover more of the past and gain some insight into the future."

"You're so certain, aren't you?"

"I am. I knew we were connected the moment I looked into your beautiful blue eyes."

"Oh, it wasn't the kiss that did it?"

"That was just confirmation." She giggled as she gently touched his hand.

⋆═◉═⋆

They finished breakfast and bathed together, once agan they couldn't keep their hands off each other. They nearly made love in the tub, but Rachel reminded him that sometimes foreplay was enough–especially when they had a schedule to keep.

Tommy obliged after a few more minutes of playing with her body–suckling her nipples, cupping her ass and sliding a few fingers inside her.

"Sorry, babe, I just can't help myself." He half-heartedly apologized.

"It will just make it that much more intense when you do get what you want. What I want too."

She kissed him and got out of the tub. He admired the curves of her wet, naked body while she dried off.

"God, Rach, you're so beautiful. I love your body."

"I can tell, fly-boy. And I love yours," she looked at him while he played with his erection. "But put that away and save it for me for later, please." Her face was glowing.

"Ugh! It's not that easy to do with you standing naked in front of me," he fretted.

"Then let me remove the temptation…" she blew him a kiss and slowly walked out of sight into the bedroom to get dressed. She knew she was driving him crazy, but she loved every minute of it, knowing what they would do to each other later.

She dressed in a sundress and hollered from the bedroom, "Okay, fly-boy, it's time for you to get some clothes on, too. We need to catch the 11:15 train to London."

"Just finishing up shaving, love. Hey, how do think I would look with a beard?"

"It would cover that handsome face, so I vote no. Come on darling."

He started to put on his uniform, but Rachel stopped him. "Tommy, *no* uniforms! This is *our* time. Let's spend them like they're the last few days of our lives and there is no war going on, okay?" He kissed her and then dressed in his civilian clothes.

⊷═◉═⊶

Settling into their seats, Tommy watched the rolling farmland on either side of the train where small herds of sheep and cattle dotted the fields. As usual, he thought of home.

He turned to Rachel. "So is Doc Cavanagh a real doctor? I mean, you met him at a carnival after all."

"Blimey, I don't know… never asked him. I've been in contact with him ever since he settled in London nearly a decade ago, give or take. I see him to help me figure out dreams or visions, and deal with other questions in my life. He has this ability to shed light on what your soul is attempting to tell you, but you can't hear. Over the years he has helped me to better understand who I am by guiding me to discover the journey my soul has been traveling. Doc even told me last spring that my great love was coming back to me."

"And you think it's me?"

"Of course, you bugger." Rachel pushed against his shoulder with her hand.

"Why do you know it's me? I mean there are a lot of people in the world. Weren't you in love with Izzy's brother?"

"Oh crikey, Tommy. It was different between me and Shelby. We had been childhood friends and I believe we had been together in a past life. When he proposed to me it just seemed the logical thing to do. I had dated other men, and he was a nice guy, but I'm not sure if he hadn't been killed we would have married. My parents had been killed in a bombing and I think I just needed to feel alive again so I said yes even though we never set a date.

"However, you and I, *we are connected* on a completely different level than I have ever experienced with any other person–male or female." Rachel turned her head, wiping a tear away while looking out the window on the other side of the train.

He realized that he had unintentionally hurt her. He put his hand on her chin while turning her head so he could see her face. "I'm sorry for making you recall all that."

"What are you questioning? Us or our love?" He heard the frustration in her voice and her baffled expression.

"No, no, no. Just that," his voice trailed off, "just that you think I'm your *one* great love, not Shelby?"

She pulled out her latest journal and thumbed through it. "Oh, here we go. The last time I saw Doc, which was just before we met, he told me at that session that you would be here soon; that he saw it in the cards, and that I would know instantly because we have been together before. He told me that the task before us is to unlock the meaning of true love.

"He said that our love is a gift from the Masters... a reward which shows that even death cannot overcome the depth of this love. There will be pain that is as great as the love. I'm hoping he's wrong about the last part. Obviously." She looked away from him again, trying to hide the fear that was difficult to disguise on her face.

Staring out the window, Tommy sat in silence as he rehashed what she'd just said while slipping his arm around her. "I hope Doc Cavanagh is wrong about the last part too." He kissed her cheek and sat back deciding to lighten the mood as he told her about life back home in the States.

The train gently rocked them back and forth and she nestled into him as he told her about his last Fourth of July, which made her laugh and put her in a good mood. He was glad they were meeting her aunt and Doc. The aroma of her hair filled his head, the softness of her skin encompassed him, all the while he wished this would be his life… forever.

Chapter 6

Tommy felt the steam engine slow to a halt as they arrived at Kings Cross Station. Getting off the train, he was unable to avoid the unmistakable signs of war; there were soldiers in uniform everywhere hurrying to board trains or loitering on benches quietly talking to each other. Tommy caught himself before saluting a few times out of habit. The station was chaotic as people scurried around dragging their children to catch trains, while others said tearful good-byes to soldiers, perhaps for the last time.

The damage to the roof of the station was unmistakable and made him realize the destruction *his* bombs brought to other cities. The mangled parts of the roof lay along the tracks to the far side of the station where laborers were stacking bricks from the wall that had caved in from the explosion. The large clock on the wall of the station still held the exact time of the destruction. He stopped as the impact of the war and his part in it hit him. Hit him hard.

"This way, Tommy." Rachel took his hand and guided him through the mass of soldiers at the train station. "It's a short hackney ride to Aunt Marilyn's flat." Rachel knew it was a quick jaunt, but hoped it would be just long enough to get Tommy's mind off the soldiers he saw at the train station. Sadly, once inside the carriage, Tommy couldn't avoid seeing the ravages of the war.

An elderly couple, the man's arm around his wife, stood in front of their home seemingly paralyzed by the destruction. Others were digging through the rubble searching for bits and pieces of their lives while children played in the bombed-out buildings. Food lines that snaked around the block for war rations were filled with forlorn looking people that reminded him of the Depression as a child, and the look of despair in his mother's face.

His stomach turned at seeing destroyed buildings, crumbled and empty, knowing the ruin was caused from a bomb. *This is what happens when bombs are dropped on a city.* He couldn't help but feel disgusted with himself as if he was personally responsible for the same damage in a different city, despite the fact that it was a necessary evil to win the war. He wished he never had to wear a uniform again.

The hackney pulled up to the curb of an apartment building on Percy Street. Tommy emotionally gathered himself and paid the fare. They walked up the short flight of stairs and Rachel buzzed her aunt's flat. Aunt Marilyn's voice boomed through the intercom and she unlocked the building door so that they could enter. They met her at the door on the second floor. She was full of smiles and hugs for both of them.

Aunt Marilyn was a short, hefty woman with faded, dyed-red hair and hazel eyes. Her teeth were stained yellow from all the tea and cigarettes she'd consumed over the years, yet she had a smile that was sweet and soothing.

Her tiny flat was filled with furniture from the Victorian age, like Rachel's cottage. The couch had quaint floral pillows and doilies covered its sagging arms. There was a sewing machine prominently displayed on a small table, and dainty figurines and other knickknacks atop every surface. But it was the photos that lined the walls of The Flying Wallendas that caught his attention along with other high wire acts from the circus. He stood there studying each of the pictures. He was totally lost while Rachel and her aunt carried on.

"Aunt Marilyn, something smells wonderful!" Rachel inhaled deeply.

Although they were meeting her for lunch, it smelled like freshly baked cookies in a bakery. Aunt Marilyn turned to Tommy, "Oh, that's dessert. If you're a good boy and clear your plate…" she jokingly scolded him with her hands on her hips. "So you're the fly-boy who stole my niece's heart? Go on, let me take a look at ya." She eyed him up and down before she giggled.

She turned to Rachel, "I think he'll do just fine, honey."

"Aunt Marilyn! You're bloody well full of spit and vinegar today, aren't you?"

"You wouldn't want me any other way."

Tommy felt as if the wind was knocked out of him when he recognized a photo from Baraboo, Wisconsin.

"So where are you from, Tommy?"

Aunt Marilyn's question had him baffled and at a loss for words. He pointed to one of the photos. "Right here."

"Baraboo, Wisconsin? Well, that's a bloody oddity if I ever heard one!" She turned back to Rachel and winked, "Like I said, he's a keeper."

"Did you live in Baraboo, Aunt Marilyn?" Rachel asked.

"Oh, yes."

"When?" Tommy leaned against the back of the couch and Rachel joined him.

"Well, let's see, I was ten years old and my parents were aerial artists and did a couple of seasons with the Ringling Brothers around, um, it must have been 1902 or 1903. We returned to London when my father was injured and could no longer perform, but he continued to work with the Wallendas."

"Fascinating."

"Which part? That I come from a family of aerialists or that we share a hometown?"

"Both really."

"Tommy, we're real proud of our accomplishments as aerialists. I was a high flyer for thirty years working with each of those acts… until my hips gave out. Hence the early retirement." She laughed at herself. "Guess we have that in common, too."

"What's that?" He was slightly confused by her comment.

"We both like being high in the sky." Aunt Marilyn stared directly into his eyes. "There's nothing like it."

"Isn't that the truth?" Tommy smiled softly. "Do you ever miss it?"

"Miss performing or Baraboo?"

"The Big Top." He could see where Rachel's wit came from.

"Always, that is until my hips act up. Then, no, not so much. Hey, let's eat, the main course is ready."

Rachel helped her aunt bring in the bangers and mash with two gravy bowls to her tiny dining room table that was already set for three, while Tommy filled the cups with tea.

As they ate the delicious lunch, Aunt Marilyn brought up their plans for the rest of the day. "So you're going to see ole Doc Cavanagh after you leave here. He's a hoot!"

"You've met him?" Tommy asked pensively in between bites.

"*Met* him? I've *known* him nearly half a century! He is a very interesting man. We've spent many hours together over countless years. He has often provided me with important insights about life. Whatever it is that he does, he's good at it! Being British, that says a lot." She laughed again.

"So how did you meet?"

"I knew him from when I worked the smaller carnivals back when he was a sideshow act. And now look at him—he's booked all the time! He traveled a lot during his younger years, mostly in Egypt if memory serves. Oh well, I'm beginning to ramble. Tell me more about you, Tommy."

"There's not much to tell. I grew up in Baraboo-"

"Don't you just love that town? I remember all the-"

"Auntie, you asked him a question," Rachel sweetly scolded her aunt.

"Pardon me, Tommy. My manners have gone away from me. Speaking of which, mind if I smoke while you finish eating?"

"Not at all, Aunt Marilyn."

⋅►══◑◖══◄⋅

When lunch was over and the cookies were eaten, Rachel and Tommy readied themselves for their three p.m. appointment with Doc Cavanagh. Aunt Marilyn put together a goodie bag of cookies for Doc and sent them with Rachel and Tommy.

Along the way to his flat, which was only three blocks over on Rathborne Street, Rachel asked Tommy what he thought of her favorite aunt.

"I think she's swell. Was she your mom's or dad's sister?"

"She's my mom's sister." She giggled.

"What's so funny, love?"

Stopping and turning to him, "Well, aren't you wondering if my mom was in the circus?"

He laughed out loud. "Actually, yes, but I was not sure if it was okay to ask."

"Yes, she was." They continued down the street. "She was a clown. She had this costume that my father hid once she retired and they opened the pub."

"Why did he hide it?

"He didn't want the townsfolk to know. Yet she would sneak it out when my father was working at the pub and put it on, sometimes with full makeup, and chase me around the house." Her laugh turned into a sigh, "I miss her Tommy!"

He slipped his arm around her. "Sorry, babe."

She quickly changed the subject "Most people think Aunt Marilyn's odd."

"I don't think *she* is odd, I think it's *odd* that she once lived in the tiny town of Baraboo, my hometown, a town that no one has ever heard of. It's interesting because she was your mom's older sister, right?"

"Yes, actually she's a stepsister, because my grandfather remarried and had three more children. My mom was the baby."

"If your grandfather hadn't gotten injured and he stayed in Baraboo, do you realize we possibly would have met there and grown up together?"

"That's a crazy thought, Tommy. It sure makes the world feel smaller."

"But to answer your question, I found her a delight. Thank you for sharing her with me."

"My pleasure, love." Rachel smiled up at him and squeezed his hand. "Say, would you mind if we wander into my favorite boutique?"

"Of course not, lead the way."

They entered the boutique and he watched as Rachel flitted about like a butterfly on flowers between each rack of clothing. Each piece was one of a kind. Some were simple, some were gaudy and cheeky. Finally, Tommy saw an unmistakable look on Rachel's face and he knew she found what she wasn't even looking for.

He took the ensemble from her hand and held the green silk outfit in front of himself.

"You should try it on, my love, because it's just not my size."

"Oh, stop! I couldn't. It's much too expensive. I just like to window shop and dream… maybe I can get Aunt Marilyn to teach me how to sew so I could make one. It would be much-"

"Rach, then we should never have come in."

He let her see how serious he was, so she gave in and neared the fitting room.

"Please try it on and see if you like the way it looks. I love the color. It suits you."

"I want it to more than suit me!"

"Get in there, you sassy Brit!"

"If you insist, sir." She halfheartedly bowed to him.

Rachel disappeared behind the curtain and the sales clerk helped her into the two-piece floral emerald green silk outfit and light brown-colored beaded headband. Luckily her brown ankle boots complemented the look and she pulled back the curtain to show Tommy her ensemble, just as the assistant handed her a light brown with umbrella that had green leaves that highlighted all the colors and brown accents throughout the two-piece garment.

Tommy caught his breath. Rachel looked stunning.

"What do you think?" she asked pensively.

"I think I love it. And we'll take the umbrella too."

"Tommy! It's much too-"

"Do you feel as beautiful as you look?"

"I do feel wonderfully glamorous." She bashfully responded while twirling around in the mirror.

"Then we have nothing left to discuss. But if you want to get to our appointment, I suggest you wear it, my love. You look beautiful in it."

"Thank you. A thousand thank yous!"

Tommy was overwhelmed by the damage to the homes and businesses along their walk to Doc Cavanagh's.

They turned onto Rathborne Street which was a row of houses. Doc Cavanagh's place was both business and home–he lived upstairs above his office.

They were a few minutes early when they walked in and heard the bells jingle from above the door. Tommy was surprised by the objects located throughout and didn't know where to look.

The décor was unmistakably Egyptian. A statue of the sphinx was the first thing he saw, followed by a painting of the Eye of Horus that took up most of one wall. There was more than one cat statue and even a few live felines roamed freely. A "death" or "mummy's mask" was sitting atop the little potbelly stove used to warm the room in winter.

He was fascinated by a strangely shaped knot of rope that was on the wall. Sitting on the leather loveseat in the waiting room, Tommy asked, "What is that?"

"That's the Knot of Isis, it represents the Goddess of Mystery. Perfect for this place, don't you think?" Rachel smiled at him.

"I don't know what I think," he replied with a sigh. "It's awfully dark in here."

"Don't worry, your eyes will adjust. He's been keeping the blackout rule in the daytime as well as nighttime. I guess I should have prepared you for the décor, sorry."

Although Tommy believed there was more to life than one time around, it seemed totally different to discuss it when faced with artifacts that he found so unfamiliar and almost intimidating.

They sat together on the loveseat holding hands while waiting for Doc to appear. The sound of chimes filled the air and the waterfall in the corner was soothing as it bubbled. The oil lamps burning incense added to the ambiance of the front room.

"He calls this the relaxation area. Feeling relaxed yet?" Rachel asked, knowing he hadn't relaxed one bit since he walked inside.

Tommy just smiled and soaked in his surroundings. The relaxation room had many pictures of Doc Cavanagh in Egypt. The wall opposite the fireplace was a full bookcase that reached the ceiling and was filled with old books and other Egyptian artifacts.

Tommy tried to release some of his apprehensive tension with humor. "I guess he really likes Egypt. Why did he ever leave? Too hot?" He released Rachel's hand.

"Thomas! Be respectful!"

"Sorry, m'lady."

Just then one of the cats jumped onto Tommy's lap and stared him down while purring and kneading his paws. He felt his rapid heartbeat slow while he petted the orange and white four-legged feline.

After a few more minutes, he was finally beginning to enjoy the moment with the cat purring when Doc Cavanagh appeared in the doorway that led to his reading room.

Doc Cavanagh was a tall, frail man with long gray hair that he wore in a ponytail. His deep brown eyes revealed his age in years but youth in his heart. He had blue silk suspenders that held his black trousers up. His tattered white shirt was unbuttoned at the collar, yet he didn't look disheveled. Around his neck hung a pendant made from stone on a thin brown leather strap.

They stood up as Doc Cavanagh greeted Rachel with a hug and she introduced him to Tommy, who shook his hand while eyeing him somewhat cautiously.

"Oh, I almost forgot. Here's a bag of goodies from Aunt Marilyn." Rachel pulled the cookies from her purse.

"Thank you, Rachel. I will ring her later to thank her." Doc Cavanagh turned his attention to Tommy while pulling up a wooden chair in front of them. "Thomas, am I wrong by saying you have a question or two for me already?"

"Who wouldn't? Where did you get all these things? The last time I saw stuff like this it was at The Field Museum in Chicago. And what is that around your neck?" Tommy smiled at Doc, "And did you train your cats to sit on strangers' laps?"

Doc slid himself back in the chair. "Oh my, my, please slow down." He smiled while holding up his hand, gesturing him to take it easy. "You're very much an American in that you want answers to everything right away. Sometimes we must wait for an answer. But you asked some simple questions, so I'll tell you. Where to begin?"

Looking at Getty who was purring on Tommy's lap, Doc said, "As far as the felines go, they aren't trained. You were chosen. Getty was drawn to you by that which he sees that we humans can't. Now, let's move on to your other questions."

Doc pointed around the room. "First, these items are ancient Egyptian artifacts that I collected while I spent time in Egypt working with Doctor James Breasted who mentored me. I met him in 1899 when he started doing his field work in Egypt at the Fertile Crescent, and spent the next ten years with him. He was from Chicago and you're absolutely right when say you saw them in the Field Museum, for he was instrumental in ascertaining them. I respect and study the Egyptian culture for it lasted over twenty-five centuries. I spent the next twenty years of my life studying the mysteries of Egypt and other Middle Eastern cultures."

Holding the amulet between his fingers, he said, "Around my neck is an Ankh Amulet that Breasted gave me as a gift. We remained very close 'til his death in 1935. It is a symbol of life."

Tommy continued to pet Getty who had begun to purr loudly as he began his kitty stomp on his lap and finally settled in a circular position.

"Well," Doc Cavanagh turned to Rachel as he continued in his soft voice, "I see the one you've been waiting for has arrived. This reading will be good for both of you. Knowledge is splendid. Perhaps we will see what the future holds."

"Wait. How did you know this is him? I didn't tell you anything about Tommy other than his name," Rachel asked enthusiastically.

"Have you forgotten that I am a clairvoyant, Rachel?" Doc smiled. "But what I see on your faces I would need to be deaf and blind to miss; it is that of true love. Shall we enter the reading room and continue our conversation?"

Rachel turned. "Come on, fly-boy, it's time to see what our future holds, and how our past has played a part in it."

"Okay, my love." Tommy had a pensive tone in his voice.

Doc Cavanagh has a way of soothing just about anyone—no wonder Rachel was so comfortable the first night she met him. I hope this is the right thing to do. Tommy picked Getty up and placed him on the loveseat, then followed Doc and Rachel into the reading room.

Rachel kissed Tommy on the cheek as they walked into the room, while Getty the cat snuck in before Doc closed the door.

Chapter 7

Tommy, Rachel and Doc all entered the reading room which was in the back of the two-story flat. It was decorated in the same Egyptian motif.

Tommy stood there for a moment as his eyes scanned the room. The dark cherry-stained parquet floor was partially covered by a midnight blue Persian square rug with intricate designs that included silhouettes of trees, people and animals.

The lighting came from oil lamps that appeared to be medium-sized gravy bowls. The aroma of the burning oil filled the room with the scents of exotic flowers in springtime. A heavy, deep sapphire blue velvet fabric covered the window in compliance with the mandated blackout of the war.

Rachel led him to an ornate round wooden table which was in the center of the room. It had a top with a beautiful tree inlay made of shiny green and brown polished stones imbedded in a wood Tommy didn't recognize.

Around the table were three chairs. Doc sat down in a well-used eighteenth century upholstered chair, leaving for them the two worn salmon-colored leather chairs on the opposite side of the table. When they sat down, Getty quickly settled into a circular position on one of two mismatching chairs against the far wall.

The floor to ceiling shelves made up an entire wall and were filled with Doc's collection of books. Just a few feet in front of the shelves was a medium-sized, dark wood desk which was covered with more books. Next to the desk was an art deco floor lamp anchored by a wrought iron base with a glass mottled-orange shade which he thought was beautiful.

Tommy broke the silence. "Next to your desk, there—is that a statue of a Pharaoh?"

Rachel responded before Doc had a chance. "No, that's the Egyptian god Shu, the ruler of the sky, whose powers were to oversee the air, the wind, and the sunlight." She reached over and grabbed his hand.

Doc offered them a cup of tea. Rachel restrained herself from giggling as Tommy accepted his second cup of the day.

"Thank you," they said in unison.

As they sipped their tea sitting around the table Doc Cavanagh spoke, "So, Rachel and Thomas, I have decided to use Tarot cards to expedite the process, since Rachel has told me we have limited time together. Tommy, are you familiar with them?"

"I heard of them but never used them." He sipped his tea while glancing over at Rachel.

"The Tarot can aid us in encountering our higher self. The cards can be excruciatingly straightforward if you are honest in your quest. However, understand that whatever the truth is, whether it be the past or the future, it is locked within each of us, which is the higher self, or the soul as I like to refer to it."

Rachel felt Tommy's hand squeeze hers tighter, as apprehension crossed his face.

"You see, time doesn't exist for our souls, it journeys through infinite lifetimes."

"Doc," Rachel said. "We feel very connected and wonder why we knew so quickly that we loved each other. We also want to ensure that we will always be able to find each other in the future," she cleared her throat as her eyes began to tear up, "future lives, that is. I don't want to lose…" Rachel started to sob softly. Tommy put his arm around her.

Doc Cavanagh nodded, reached across the table and patted her hand. He looked at both of them and finally focused on Tommy. "Is this the information you seek as well, Thomas?"

"Yes, it is."

"Are you sure? Once we start opening the doors, they cannot be shut. You understand?" Doc's gentle expression changed to reflect how serious he was about their quest.

"I also want to know that I will be with Rachel forever, Doc. I'm so in love with her I would follow her into death just to be with her. What can I do to make our dream come true?" He looked at Doc intently.

Rachel was caught off guard and gasped slightly at his statement, placing her hand over her heart. Meanwhile Doc just picked up his cup of tea and nodded.

"Okay, then. Let's get started. I want to start by describing how we perceive the world around us. The tools we generally use as humans are our five major senses: taste, smell, sight, hearing and touch. However, we tend to rely a great deal on sight as it stimulates our brains quickly. Taste and smell could be overruled by sight because we are creatures that want what we see even if it doesn't appeal to our taste or smell.

"These human senses rule the body and influence our minds into making decisions based primarily on the assessment of what could be the truth, but may only be half-truths. For example, who doesn't want to be loved, or feel love? So we search using our five senses to lead the way, or follow the path, and we all know how that goes. At times, we settle." He leaned forward in his seat looking back and forth at them.

"So, you want to know why you connected so quickly and easily. What senses did you use when you first met?"

Rachel and Tommy looked at each other then turned to Doc and Tommy answered first.

"Well Doc, I would be lying if I said Rachel's physical beauty wasn't a factor. I couldn't stop watching her that first night at the pub. The way she moved almost cat-like; her eyes sparkled when she spoke to me; the way her lips formed words." He looked at Rachel with adoration.

"As I walked down the street I passed two other pubs where guys from the base were going. I heard the music, people laughing and talking. But for reasons I can't explain I kept walking, like I was being pulled toward her. Sounds crazy, right?"

Tommy looked at Rachel and she saw his crystal-blue eyes filled with love and desire for her.

Doc interrupted them breaking their gaze. "Thomas," Doc paused, "there are no right or wrong answers to the questions. I can sense how heartfelt you have been. And no, it doesn't sound crazy at all. For how often what we perceive to be a wrong turn was meant to be the right turn all along, and lead the way to the unexpected."

"That actually makes sense, Doc."

"Don't sound so surprised." He laughed and then turned to Rachel, "Shall we continue?" Doc put two lumps of sugar into his cup and poured tea over them from the yellow china teapot.

Rachel cleared her throat and squeezed Tommy's hand. She braced herself for a moment and then spoke. "I will be just as straightforward. As soon as I saw him, I lost my breath at how bloody handsome he is. But there have been many soldiers that I've met over the last three years that were handsome. However, there was something different about him, something *in* him that touched me deep inside. I can't explain it. I was drawn to him.

"I have never kissed someone so compulsively like I did with him the first time we met. I actually couldn't believe I even did that. Afterwards I prayed he would return because I wanted-*needed* to be near him."

Rachel's face flushed as she remembered the passion of the kiss, while Doc calmly stirred his tea. Tommy lifted her hand to his lips and kissed it.

They both sat silently as Doc centered his cup on the saucer. "So it appears that even though you were drawn together by your sense of sight to a degree, it was another sense that you have yet to discover that connects you. Is that a fair assessment in both of your opinions?"

"Yes," they both agreed.

"Rachel, since you and I have had a long-term relationship, you realize I need to delve into Thomas's life with him. So, do you mind if we have a little time alone?"

Rachel looked at Doc with surprise, but replied, "Of course not. I understand." She tried not to show her overwhelming feeling of rejection.

"Do you mind, Thomas?" Doc looked at Tommy as he waited for his answer.

"Sure, Doc. I'm fine with that."

Rachel got up from her chair, kissed Tommy on the cheek and whispered, "I love you so much." She went back into the relaxation room, closing the door behind her.

While sitting down on the loveseat she had shared with Tommy earlier, a heaviness filled her. Something had changed and she felt it deeply within her core. It reminded her of how fragile life was. "Mom…" she whispered, wishing she could talk to her, confide in her, seek her guidance.

Chapter 8

Tommy sat across the round table from Doc. Rachel's leaving made Tommy slightly uncomfortable and he joked, "So is this where you ask me about my intentions with your daughter?" Nerves rattled him.

Doc smiled while looking down into the teacup he was holding as if reading a message on the bottom. "No, no. That's none of my business." Placing the cup in the saucer he refilled it from the china teapot. "More tea, Thomas?"

He studied the lines and wrinkles on Doc's face, wondering if they were caused by the smile that seemingly never left his face.

"No, thank you, I'm fine." *Why do I feel so close to him?*

He looked at the statue right behind Doc, almost hoping it would speak. The room and the statues felt alive. He was sure they were watching him and already knew his fate.

Doc took a sip of his tea and relaxed back into his chair, folding his hands across his midsection.

"You sure have an enormous collection of books. Are you actually a doctor?"

"Would that make what you will discover today more believable?"

"Well, no, um, maybe. But honestly I was just wondering." He glanced away, embarrassed that he'd asked.

"It's fine that you inquired. Yes, I am a doctor. My degree is in anthropology, specializing in the ancient Egyptian culture. Now that we've gotten that out of the way, Thomas, I wanted to have a few moments alone so we could talk about you, not about me. I see myself as a tool to enlighten the way for others. So, how long have you had the ability to see things before they happen?"

Tommy sat there quietly for a few minutes staring at the tree on the table. *How does he know that about me?* He felt exposed thinking Rachel had told him. He looked up at Doc who was patiently waiting for him to answer.

"Doc, I'm not sure what you mean. After all, aren't you the one who can tell the future?" *Jesus Christ! Let's just get on with this reading.*

"So you just want a sideshow from the carnival and a fortune cookie that wishes you good luck? Oh, and let's see, I know you feel bad that your best friend never came home from the war. We will all remember him forever and ever, right?" Doc looked at him with cynical grin. "Oops, almost forgot, one pound please."

Tommy wondered why Doc was being so sarcastic with a matter that was so close to his heart. Couldn't he see this was tearing him apart? *You son of a bitch! Just sitting there smugly relaxing in your chair... you have no idea what I'm going through!* After another few seconds, he relaxed. *Stop being such an asshole, Tommy! It's not his fault.*

"Doc, don't you understand how I feel right now? I could be dead in the next forty-eight hours. Then I would never see her again!" He couldn't stop his eyes from filling with salty tears. "No matter what you tell me about the future, it doesn't matter since I already know it! And all you need to do is sit back and drink your fucking tea. Jesus Christ! I really need a cup of coffee right now! You act like there are a million tomorrows and there's not!"

He couldn't hold his tears back any longer and he buried his head into his arms that were folded on the round table.

Doc's hand rested on his head and immediately calm eradicated his angst. "Thomas, just keep your eyes closed and turn off all your thoughts. I'm leaving you for a few minutes."

"I'm sorry, Doc." Tommy spoke through his tears.

"Now listen, let go of the anger you are feeling and think about how life ebbs and flows much like the waves of the ocean you crossed to find yourself here."

He was still face down on his arms when he heard the door softly creak as Doc left the room. Darkness filled his thoughts. *I don't understand what they want from me! I love her so much, is that so bad?* Tommy wasn't sure if he had spoken the words or thought them.

Tommy finally sat up and looked around before going over to the statue next to Doc's desk. Putting his hand on the statue's head he said, "Well I guess things didn't go your way either, my silent friend."

He walked over to the bookcase and looked at all the different books. *The Principles of Nature, Her Divine Relations; Science and Health with Key to the Scriptures* by Mary Baker Eddy. Peering more closely at the selection, a book entitled *Heaven and Hell* caught his eye, and he laughed out loud… "Yeah, I understand that one without even reading it!"

Tommy pulled out the book by Eddy and opened it. He saw the date it was published, 1874, and gently slid the book back in its place. Turning around he saw Doc standing there watching him. "Oh, sorry Doc. I didn't realize how old these books were."

"Not a problem. They are there to be read, not to look at. I made you a pot of coffee, my friend." Holding the pot elevated in the air he said, "Let's enjoy a cup together." Doc poured out two fresh cups before sitting back down into his chair and crossing his legs. Tommy started over toward his seat but stopped when he saw a picture of a young woman on the doctor's desk.

He picked it up. "She's beautiful, Doc."

Doc nodded. "She is, and she had the most dazzling hazel eyes I had ever looked into." He softly cleared his throat. "We met in Egypt while working for Dr. Breasted on his first field project. I arrived in the Port of Alexandria on a cool day in February 1899; I think it was February 7th. Either way, I was twenty-four years old on my first trip to Egypt. I had been fascinated by the Egyptian culture my entire life." He drank his coffee with a faraway expression.

"So, what was it like to see the pyramids, Doc?" He leaned forward as Doc refilled their cups.

"The pyramids were amazing, but nothing compared to the moment I first saw her. I was in line at the terminal in port going through customs when I saw her holding a white sign against her chest with my name on it. She wore a sky-blue cotton prairie skirt with a high-necked white blouse and a floppy wide-brimmed straw hat. She was the very picture of Victorian perfection, a vision."

Doc closed his eyes with a large smile on his face. Tommy imagined he was recalling the woman's image in his mind. He sat quietly until Doc opened his eyes and took a few sips of his coffee. Love.

"Well Thomas, I think we need to get back on track here, don't you agree?"

"I suppose so, but what happened? I mean her picture's on your desk after forty years. I feel like I need to know. Please tell me what happened, Doc. You married her? Got engaged?"

"I've never told anyone, including Rachel, about her. So, this is between us, agreed?" Doc made eye contact with him as he waited for his answer.

"Never to be shared by me to anyone."

"Correct, Thomas. You can do that?"

"Yes, I can do that." He nodded and stared back into Doc's deep brown eyes.

"After I finished with customs, I approached her and she instantly stuck her delicate hand out and slipped it into mine. What electricity moved between us! She said, 'Eleanor Owens, and you are Roland Cavanagh, I imagine.' I stood there staring into her face with these hazel eyes that had brown flecks in them. Her lips moved while she spoke, and oh, the sound of her voice left me speechless, I'm not sure I understood her at first. 'Mr. Cavanagh, are you well?' I finally came to my senses and replied, 'I do apologize, Ms. Owens. I am well. I am just entranced.'"

Tommy imagined the scene, and felt Doc's emotions while he spoke as if they were his own.

"She and I worked together for Breasted for the next four months and I fell deeply in love with her. Everything about her from the smell of her hair to silly things like the way she hiccupped. Thomas, I felt unworthy of her. She was physically more beautiful than any woman I had ever known. And she was so bloody smart, my God! Doing research with her was a dream."

Doc looked at Tommy, and Tommy noticed the smile had left his face.

"You okay, Doc?"

"Yes, Thomas."

"Then what happened with you and her?"

"We were on a boat headed up the Nile to Thebes. It was a beautiful day and I finally found the nerve to reach over and take her hand. Looking into her beautiful hazel eyes, I told her how I'd felt since the day we met. I said, 'I knew we were soul mates and that's why we were both here, we were meant to be together.'

"Her reply has echoed in my mind since day she spoke it. 'Roland, I'm sorry if I have misled you regarding my feelings about you, but I return to the States next month to be married in December.' She told me she had never spoken of her fiancé since we've been so wrapped up in our work. We had been so excited to be involved in such wonderful research about Egyptian beliefs—the power of the third eye, radiating beyond our wildest imaginations. She hoped we could remain friends because I understood her like no one else."

Doc got up and walked over to his desk, looking at her picture before rustling through one of his drawers. Tommy watched as he gently handled an old, yellowed envelope.

"You came here seeking answers, Thomas. We don't always get what we want and in this envelope is why we must listen to our souls. I am going to use the loo while you read what is in the letter." Doc opened the door and left the room.

Tommy held the letter in his hand, the paper crinkly and yellowed. He pulled the letter out of the old envelope and noticed it was postmarked December 21, 1910.

He read the beautiful handwriting.

My Dearest Roland. During the last ten years, there has not been a day that I haven't regretted not following my soul that day on the Nile. Especially after all we learned about the soul guiding us while working together; however, fear held me back.

A couple of weeks ago I met a man named Edgar Cayce who regressed me, my mind's eye, you might say. In that regression, you and I were together in a different time and place, but I knew it was you the minute I looked into your eyes. Please forgive me for such mistrust of my heart. I pray that you never stop helping others, for you have a beautiful gift–you are blessed with the gift of intuitiveness.

I recently spent some time with Dr. Breasted and he told me you were an incredible archaeologist and will be missed since you were leaving his team. I feel that I have never left you since I work at the Field Museum and continue to work on the Fertile Crescent displays. You are everywhere I look.

I should have reached out to you over the last decade since we were together, but I couldn't because I never wanted to cause you additional pain. I write to you now because Mr. Cayce told me I needed to reach out to you before I leave. You see my sweet soul, I wish we could have made more memories together as a couple. But now as I'm dying from consumption, I beg of you to look for me on the other side when you get there. I could already be gone by the time this letter arrives. My love, I will be waiting for you on the other side.

Goodnight and farewell, your devoted love, forever and ever, Ellie.

Doc returned to the room and sat back in his chair. "Well Thomas, thank you for sharing this with me. You were looking at the books that load my bookshelves, filled with information about philosophy, facts and truths. But my biggest truth is within that small frame that sits on my desk. Please understand I'm not diminishing the value of books. But I have discovered there is more truth written in our souls."

The doctor relaxed in his seat, his face appeared to be glowing. "Doc, what happened to Ellie?"

"She died December 25, 1910."

Both men sat in silence, the barriers between them dissipated. At that moment, they shared an understanding of each other's journey.

Chapter 9

August 11, 1944 – 3:33 p.m.

Rachel felt like a prisoner in the vestibule and found it difficult and ironic that she couldn't relax in the relaxation room. She heard Doc and Tommy talking in the reading room. One of the cats rubbed against her legs and caused her to jump. She sat nervously on the loveseat with the cat on her lap—a welcome but momentary distraction. She kept thinking of her mother and wished she could talk to her.

Feeling almost trapped, she went over to the door leading into the reading room. Like a child, she placed her ear against the door hoping to be able to eavesdrop on what Tommy and Doc were talking about. She wanted to be a fly on the wall to actually hear what they were saying. Their muffled voices were driving her insane—it reminded her of being a youngster when she was forced to stay in her room and not witness the adult conversations.

She resented being left out of the conversation in the other room as she paced back and forth between the front door and the reading room. Finally, she pushed the door and went outside; a gentle breeze whipped through her hair and kissed her face. It made her feel like she was being touched by her mother's spirit.

Rachel had been close to both of her parents when they were alive, but she could tell her mother anything. Now, more than ever, she wished she could tell her mother about Tommy.

After pacing back and forth outside along the street, she went in and decided to write a letter to her mother in her journal. She scribbled feverishly.

Mom! I miss you so bloody much! I wish you were here. I can't shake this dreadful feeling… it's as if I <u>know</u> I'm going to lose him! Him! You have no idea who he is… it's not Shelby, I loved him, yes, but oh, I now know what true love is. I wish you were here to meet him. You and

Daddy would approve of him, even though he's an American pilot. You would like him, I just know it. I love him so very much. He's my other half. I wish I could just tell him not to fly—ever again. What would my life be like without him? I can't bear the thought. I've already lost so many pieces of my heart to this bloody war and I don't think I can handle another devastating loss. Losing Tommy would break me, destroy my heart.

Tears rolled over her cheek as she continued to write.

Right now, I feel helpless. The love of my life, my lives, is in the next room and I can't even go in and touch him until they invite me back in. This time is precious and being apart is a completely nonsensical waste of time!

Just then another one of Doc's cats jumped up onto her lap, covering her journal and purring loudly. She took a breath and gave in to the comfort and warmth the animal gave her. Putting down her journal she stroked the black and white cat. Eventually her anxiety slowed, as well as her heartbeat.

◦→═◎═←◦

Tommy saw the smile return to Doc's eyes as he replaced the letter inside the envelope. He was surprised when Doc asked the question again. "So, how long have you had the ability to see things before they happen?"

Tommy shrugged and looked down at the tree on the table. Doc had become a man, a possible friend, Roland. "Can I ask you one more question before I answer that question?"

"Sure."

"Did you ever find someone else?" Tommy saw a hint of sadness reach Doc's eyes.

"I never made room for anyone else. I always dreamed that she would return to continue our quest to uncover the ancient mysteries of life. My work opened my third eye to understanding our existence." Doc clapped his hands and laughed. "Enough about me. Take a moment and think back to when you first discovered this gift of seeing."

Tommy closed his eyes and instantly knew the answer. His voice was almost a yell as he blurted, "I was ten years old."

"Tell me how you discovered it." Doc leaned toward him, inviting confidences.

Tommy laughed lightly in remembrance. "An elderly Indian man named Sky Bear taught me how to listen to the "invisible world" as he called it. He referred to it as the voice of the great spirit that was in all creatures, and that this gift would guide me if I allowed it."

He looked at Doc, who sank back in his chair with his hands on his lap. "He was a lot like you, now that I think about it. The fact that you and Aunt Marilyn are friends is so odd, but it almost makes sense now. She lived in Baraboo where this story actually happened—it's kind of strange."

Doc showed little expression, but Tommy felt his kindness as if the emotion was tangible. "It is a small world and there are no coincidences. Tell me the rest of the story, Thomas."

"I've mentioned that I grew up in a small town in Wisconsin named Baraboo? Well, my younger brother Robert and I used to go camping during the summer months around Devil's Lake. One night I was telling him a scary campfire story about a young Ho Chunk Indian princess, which was the name of the local Indian tribe. She fell in love with a French hunter she met in the woods one day but explained to him that she was betrothed to another."

"Campfire stories!" Doc rubbed his hands together.

"The young French hunter made friends with her father, the chief, and he eventually expressed his desire to marry the princess and asked for his blessing. The young brave who had also asked for her hand in marriage protested. So, to settle the dispute, the chief told the two suitors that whoever returned first with an eaglet from the nest that was on the other side of the lake in a large pine tree could have her hand in marriage.

"The young Frenchman got to the nest first and had the eaglet in hand." Tommy held out his hand, palm up. "But the young brave, filled with anger over losing, broke the limb beneath the foot of the Frenchman causing him to fall. The princess heard her name as he screamed it while he fell to his death. She immediately ran to the lake to swim across it to be at his side, but she disappeared beneath the water never to be seen again."

"Tragic. But how is it scary?"

"On the night of a full moon their spirits roam the water searching for each other, and can be heard on the lake." Tommy shivered, having heard the mournful sounds for himself.

"And how does that lead you to Sky Bear?"

"Well, there we were—two kids, eight and ten years old camping under a *full moon* when suddenly we heard someone moaning. It came from the direction of the lake. I knew it was just a story, but you can imagine how scared my young brother was.

"Robert and I grabbed our Boy Scout flashlights to go investigate the noises. We found an older man, who was known around town by the name of Sky Bear, lying on the small beach along the shore. He asked us to help him up since he had twisted his ankle badly after a canoeing accident on the lake. Of course, we agreed, and between us we helped him back to our campsite."

He paused, uncertain about how to continue. "It is just so strange, the ending…" He'd spent most of his life denying what happened.

Doc touched the amulet at his neck. "Please let me hear the story and judge for myself whether or not it is strange."

"Okay. During the next couple of years whenever I went camping alone, Sky Bear would meet up with me deep in the woods and teach me the Ho Chunk ways. He would teach me to open my mind and listen to my inner voice, the "wanagi tacaku" he called it. He told me that I once was one of the sky people of his tribe and I have the inner voice and that it will reveal to me the past, present and future.

"He told me unfortunately humans place more trust in the knowledge that they have been taught through the five senses and in books to guide them in life. They have forgotten what their ancestors used to survive, the "wanagi tacaku" for guidance.

"The last time I saw him I was about thirteen, he came to say good-bye to me. I cried, Doc. He called me Little Bear and told me to close my eyes. I saw his face and then him walking away. When I opened my eyes, he was gone.

"Doc, since Sky Bear taught me I have listened to my inner voice to guide me. It's become instinctual. Although at times, I don't always follow it. Human nature, I suppose." Tommy laughed through his thick throat.

Doc gently smiled at Tommy. "Do you know what "wanagi tacaku" actually means?"

"Isn't it basically intuition?" He'd never actually researched it.

"Thomas, the English translation is the spirit path."

Tommy nodded. "That makes sense."

"So what does your intuition tell you your future holds?"

Tommy thought quietly for a moment and then he began to cry. Deep sorrow was ahead and there was nothing he could do about it but accept.

Doc reached over the table and grabbed Tommy's hands, holding them tightly. They looked at each other and Tommy sighed, then started to laugh.

"Thank you for sharing that intimate story with me. You have given me great insight as to who you are." Doc smiled, not lessening his grip. "When you gather yourself, I think it's time to bring Rachel back in."

Rachel. The reason he was here. "Yes."

Doc released his hands and Tommy wiped his tears with his palm. He took a deep breath and got up from his chair to get Rachel. As soon as he opened the door to the vestibule, Rachel jumped up from the loveseat and wrapped her arms around him while kissing his face.

"Darling, I love you."

Tommy hugged her back and whispered, "Rach, I more than love you. Thank you for suggesting this, I'm glad you wanted me to meet Doc. He is an amazing human being."

"Wow. Will you tell me what took you so long?"

"I'll tell you later. But again, thank you, my love."

They both walked back into the reading room, but Doc wasn't there. They sat down in their chairs. "So, what did you two talk about?"

Her question caught him off guard because of what Doc had told him about Ellie. His mind was a bit scattered. "Well a lot things. I told him a story from when I was a kid."

Noticing his manner, "What kind of a story was that?" She focused on him intensely as if she felt he was hiding something from her.

Tommy shrugged. "It was just about growing up in Wisconsin. Babe, relax…"

Just then the door opened and Doc walked into the room with a freshly made pot of tea and three new cups. He smelled of cigarettes and Tommy, who usually didn't smoke, found himself suddenly craving one. Doc placed the cups on their empty saucers, filling two cups with tea. He poured Tommy a coffee from the carafe already on the table.

"Rachel," Doc said as he sat down in his chair and began adding sugar to his steaming cup, "May I interrupt you before you start an inquisition on what Thomas and I spoke about?"

She blushed at his comment and Tommy found it endearing. "Sure Doc, it's just my curiosity getting the best of me." Rachel poured some milk and sugar into her cup of tea.

"Let's finish the questions you asked me earlier. Why you were drawn to each other so quickly and how you will know each other in the future. Because the answer is the same—if you remember to use the power within to guide you." He paused, acknowledging them with a nod. "Both of you have learned an important skill."

Tommy couldn't imagine what it might be that they'd each learned. He and Rachel were so different.

Doc reached into his shirt pocket and pulled out a crumpled U.S. one dollar bill, splaying it flat, he placed it face down on the table. "So, what picture do you see on the left side of the bill?"

They both looked. "A pyramid with an eye on it," Rachel answered.

"Thomas, do you know what they call that eye?"

"The all-seeing eye of God? You have a form of it in the front room. It's quite impressive, by the way."

Rachel reached over to rest her hand on Tommy's. Immediately, his tension eased.

"Thank you. Look at it as the gate that leads to higher consciousness. People who have this capacity to utilize their third eye are sometimes known as seers or "sky people." However, as I said before, the body is only the framework that houses a part of man which is called the soul. I call the body causal as the soul leaves us upon death to seek a new place to exist. The soul within us houses the history of each life it has experienced, all of which is available for us to use, if we so choose. You both have been lucky enough to have been shown how to retrieve the information that is stored in the third eye." He tapped the bill.

Tommy lifted their clasped hands to his lips and kissed her hand. They smiled at each other. *How?*

Doc continued, "It is what gives you the ability to know that you have been together before, and can be in the future. The eye allows your soul to see. Therefore, your souls recognized each other from the past."

Rachel cried quiet tears and Tommy gently rubbed her arm with his other hand.

"So, Doc, what you're saying is we will always be able to find each other?" And lose each other. Was that why Rachel was crying?

"I believe so and you need to trust that your souls, and the Masters, will not let you down in the future. I wish we had more time but we should now move on with the Tarot cards and delve into the present and the future. Who wants to go first?"

Tommy was slightly reluctant and hoped chivalry masked his fear-laden response. "Ladies first."

Chapter 10

Rachel stared at the cards as Doc Cavanagh shuffled—
what would he reveal that she didn't already sense? Time
was short.

"All right my darling, down to business. Pick six
random cards from the deck." He spread them out before
her.

Rachel did as she was told and picked six cards from
the tarot deck.

Doc Cavanagh turned the first one over.

"Your first card represents how you feel about
yourself. Lucky, you, it is the Lovers. And it is facing

upwards; therefore, it is not blocked, so love is free flowing and true. This new relationship has brought you much joy. But there are always surprises–good and bad."

Rachel sighed and squeezed Tommy's hand. He smiled in return.

"Doc, I'm going to take notes." She retrieved her journal from her bag. "I don't want to forget anything and this way I can revisit the reading from time to time."

"As you wish, my dear."

Tommy held on to her chair as she pulled out the journal and placed it on her lap so that she didn't disturb the cards. Rachel feverishly wrote on the pages. "Okay, I am ready."

Doc continued, "Your second card is not blocked either, it is what you want most right now, and it is the Tower. This means you are probably looking for an easy solution for a difficult situation. However, in life, turmoil and upheaval often bring about positive changes, just not quite the way we would like it. It is time to seize the opportunity that is forcing change as a chance for a new beginning regardless of the outcome."

"The war! The bloody war!" she mumbled while writing. Her fear of losing Tommy overwhelmed her and she tried to hide it, but her hands were trembling. Her handwriting was almost illegible.

Doc flipped over her third card. "The next card represents your fears and it is blocked, this means it will be difficult to achieve. It is the Emperor. Your success is just around the corner, in whatever form you define success, but it remains just out of reach. You may be concerned that the support and help you want from your father, husband or partner or yet even another man of significance in your life won't materialize. Trust and ask for the help you need and success will be yours, Rachel. Remember though, you will need to exercise every bit of your energy to reach your goal. You may need time for this to happen."

Rachel's tears streamed down her face as she absorbed what Doc said. Her heart was breaking out of fear of losing him. It seemed surreal to acknowledge her greatest fear–losing him–in front of Doc and Tommy. But she couldn't utter a word about it. She hurriedly wiped her tears away while she jotted his words in her journal. Tommy tenderly rubbed her back, with his strong hands, lending her assurance with a simple touch.

"Your fourth card represents what is going *for* you at the moment and it is the Fool. It is not blocked. The fool means you have an exciting time ahead of you for fun and wonderful experiences. Your confidence should be high. It's a great opportunity for new possibilities. If you are considering leaving your job, home or relationship, you will. An unexpected desire will be fulfilled even before you express it."

"But how does that work with the Emperor? How am I supposed to get what is waiting just around the bloody corner and then leave everything as a fool would?"

"Rachel, darling, you know the cards tell the truth. They can be interpreted in many ways. I merely speak the truth of the cards. You pulled them. They're trying to tell you something. If we can continue, maybe this will make sense?"

Wiping her tears of frustration, she wrote while nodding her head in agreement. When she was finished, he flipped the next card.

"Your fifth card represents what is going against you, and you pulled Justice. It is blocked. It generally means things just aren't going your way or you are the victim of foul play. You won't win this one. Heed the advice you hear and be aware of being motivated solely by self-interest."

"That one doesn't make sense to me at all, Doc. Unless…" Rachel's voice trailed off… *I'm going to lose him to this war.*

"Sometimes, as you know, the realization of the cards is not understood immediately, but in the future."

Rachel sighed deeply. "Well, I bloody hell don't like the direction of that card, but okay. What's next?" Another heavy sigh escaped her as Doc flipped the final card.

He smiled down at the image. "Your final card is the World. It represents the likely outcome. This card is not blocked, therefore the outcome may be immediate. It represents success, fulfillment and conclusion are near at hand. The successful outcome in a relationship and your efforts are rewarded. You may decide to act upon a wonderful and fulfilling relationship offered. I suggest you enjoy every moment."

Doc's smile faded when he looked at Rachel. Tears clouded her vision, and she accepted his clean handkerchief. What did it all mean?

"Rachel, do you have further questions at this point?"

Too many to get answered, she thought while she shook her head no; she was unable to speak while she wiped her tears and runny nose. She continued to write in her journal, knowing that she would study it over and over until everything made sense to her.

"Then I suggest before we begin Thomas's reading, we take a break and stretch our legs."

During their break, Rachel reviewed her notes, and added more thoughts as they came to her. Tommy enjoyed watching her nose scrunch in concentration. He pet Getty, who flipped over for a belly rub. There was so much to think about that he focused on the feel of fur beneath his fingers instead of attempting to analyze the cards Rachel had drawn.

◦⇥⟫◯⟪⇤◦

Before long, Doc Cavanagh returned from his apartment upstairs to continue with their reading and further discussion. He smelled of a freshly finished cigarette, and this time Tommy asked if he could have one.

"Doc, do you mind if I have one of your smokes? I'm a little nervous about my reading."

"Of course not. But you will disturb Sir Getty and he has taken a shine to you. You are one of the few. He's usually scarce when it comes to readings."

"What do you think that means, Doc? I'm not trying to read into everything that happens, but I can't help it." The room invited mysteries.

"For starters, Thomas, his belly is exposed. That means he trusts you."

"I didn't know that. What else?"

Doc laughed. "Beyond that, I really can't say. I'm into the human psyche, not the felines. Follow me and we'll enjoy a ciggy together. Rachel, would you like one?"

"I think I would."

They followed Doc as he pulled aside the blue velvet blackout curtains and walked through the French doors to a patio area. The modest patio had a cobblestone floor. A small fountain gurgled quietly on the wall and made the outdoor space feel cozy even though it was unadorned. They sat around the wrought iron table on bistro chairs.

"Would you like a nip of brandy?" Doc offered.

"Why, yes, that would be splendid," Rachel answered aloud and Tommy nodded in agreement.

The trio enjoyed a cigarette and brandy avoiding any talk of the war by talking about the warmer than usual August weather. The break was just what Tommy needed to gather his courage and face his future, according to the cards.

⊷⊜⊶

Back inside, they each settled into their respective seats, including Getty on Tommy's lap. Doc announced with a smile, "Let us begin." He shuffled the cards and had Tommy shuffle the cards again, to put his own energy into them, and then instructed him to choose six cards.

Doc kept the cards face down in the order that Tommy chose them. Rachel was anxious as Doc flipped the first one.

"The first card represents how you feel about yourself. You happened to choose the Devil."

Rachel gasped and turned her gaze to Tommy, who wore a questionable expression. "What does this mean?" he asked, his cheeks flushing.

"Now don't get bloody freaked out, it has many meanings. Plus there is not a block on this card, meaning you have a clear path for the most righteous way. One of the possible reasons for pulling this card is you feel that the temptation of a certain relationship, past life, or other form of pleasure is too hard to resist. It's easier to listen to the sweet promises of immediate gratification without weighing results."

"Rachel is very addictive!" He put her hand to his mouth to nip her knuckles. "Doc, I couldn't get her out of my mind from the moment I met her. I'm beginning to believe she's right when she says we've been together before."

He is finally getting it. She scribbled notes about the card and Tommy's reply in her journal.

"I understand how you feel about her and that is all good and well. But you need to question the decisions that you might make, based on those emotions. Those sorts of decisions can create a mixture of good and bad results which could possibly influence your future happiness."

"Oh, dear." Her heart skipped a beat.

Doc continued, "You may also have rather low self-esteem now and feel that there's not much hope for the future. So, you begin to doubt your ability about making good assessments. Try to be more positive and think carefully and clearly about the outcome."

Rachel was petting his hand when he suddenly ignited into an uncontrollable rage as he stood up toppling his chair back with a force that sent Getty flying. "WELL, FUCK ME!" He screamed feeling like his brain was going to explode.

Both Rachel and Doc were caught off guard as they just sat there watching him. She instinctively needed to protect him and she stood up putting her arms around him. "My sweet Tommy, it's okay. I love you. Please, love, it's all well and fine, I'm right here."

"I'm sorry." He said in wispy voice trying to control his rapid breathing. Lifting his chair off the floor they all settled back down as Doc began again.

"Apparently I hit a nerve, Thomas?" Doc stared at him cautiously.

"Yes, sir. I would do anything to spend the rest of my days on earth with Rachel. Anything. I would even go AWOL for her."

Rachel dropped her pen and looked up from her journal. She had been writing so quickly she could have been a stenographer in court. "Tommy! My love! I will be here when you finish your tour. I'm not going anywhere. Besides, you wouldn't be able to live with yourself!"

"What if I die before there is a chance to spend the rest of our lives together, Rach?" It was impossible for him to hide his sadness from her.

Tears filled her eyes. "Tommy, please don't ever bloody talk like that again!" Rachel grabbed his arm, alarmed because deep down they each feared the same thing.

⁂

"I think we should continue with the next card." Doc interrupted the emotional scene between Tommy and Rachel.

"Sorry, Rach." He kissed her cheek feeling foolish for having thoughts of going AWOL. "I'm ready, Doc."

"Your next card represents what you may want most right now. It is the Hierophant. It is not blocked. Before I tell you what this card means, you should understand that a hierophant represents a person who interprets mysteries of esoteric principles; a person for whom you have high respect. It is believed that they have been chosen to share their gift of wisdom."

"That would be you then." He sincerely felt the same aura and spirit of Sky Bear in Doc. Getty jumped back onto his lap and purred loudly while kitty-stomping on his legs.

"I am honored by that, and I honor you. *Namaste.*"

"*Namaste?* What does that mean?"

"Basically, the God in me honors the God in you."

"I like that."

"Back to the meaning of the card, Thomas, which is almost ironic at this point: By pulling the Hierophant, it means that you want to have someone around you that you trust and can confide in, knowing that they won't let you down or judge you. The card speaks loudly of moral issues here, such as knowing right from wrong. It may be that you want some advice or wise counsel from a teacher, priest, parent or someone with whom you have a lot of respect for to help you make the right decision. I don't know what else I can say to you about this card. It almost speaks for itself after what you've said."

"I believe you covered it. You said it wasn't blocked, right?"

"Correct."

Rachel was writing every word in her journal. Would she feel good that he'd sought Doc's help in making decisions?

"That's good enough for me. Next?" Tommy spoke with slight impatience. Doc turned the next card over.

"The third card is the Moon. It represents your fears and once again it is not blocked. It means that lies and insecurity are likely to be prominent in your life at the moment. You are afraid of being deceived and afraid that you are being misled. Trust your instincts and let them guide you away from those who are in control.

"Your turbulent emotions are muddying the waters. Step back and try to find clarity of mind. Although this task may seem difficult, the moon helps to illuminate the darkness. It will turn out alright in the end.

"Any question about this?"

He would need time to mull it all over. Tommy shook his head no, but Rachel blurted, "I have a million questions!"

"Rachel," Doc sweetly scolded her, "It's not an open discussion."

"I know. I bloody well know I can't interfere. But I want to!"

Doc smiled at her and moved on to the fourth card. "Thomas, your next card is what is going *for* you, and you pulled the Empress, yet it is blocked. Which again, that means you must work extra hard to make your desires align with your intentions. The card generally means the harvest has arrived and you are entering a cycle of abundance, happiness and joy. Your creative energy is high, so if you are considering starting a family, a new job or artistic endeavor, this is a favorable time."

"Okay." Tommy winked at Rachel. He so wanted to marry her and hoped it would happen despite the block on this card. He knew by her meek smile at him that she too, was having doubts about the particular card.

"Your next card represents what is going against you. It is the Hermit. It means you are at risk of doing something hasty out of impatience and rage, and it is not blocked. This is not a time for irrational or impulsive behavior. Do not be arrogant or resentful. Try to remain calm and let go of your rage. Take time to make cool and collected decisions. This card signals a warning not to take hasty actions."

Tommy's career as a pilot was to make calm, quick decisions. And despite his anger he would never hurt Rachel. Doc was off on this one.

"Thomas, if I may add, your volatile emotion keeps popping up in the cards. Do you have any questions?"

"No. I follow my instincts while I fly with *FiFi*."

"*FiFi?*" Doc asked.

"She's my B-17, *Fifinella*."

"Bless *FiFi*," Rachel said to herself as she quietly wrote everything down. His reading was tearing her up inside again as she continued to write.

"Yes, let us bless *FiFi* so that she may be one with you, Thomas."

"Thank you."

"Your sixth card is the likely outcome, Justice. No block. Decisions will go in your favor, particularly regarding partnerships. Now is the time for some good luck and rewards for your honorable deeds in the past."

He sighed in relief that it was his last card. It was all very intense. It seemed that every card he pulled spoke to him about either the relationship he was in with Rachel or him being a soldier during WWII. He only wondered how much longer he would be a soldier, for he knew she would always be his one true love.

"Thomas, this was just a card reading. Understand that there is much more for us to uncover, you have been given a lot to sort through. I suggest we stop here for now and wait until the next time we are together for more. When you reflect on our time we spent here today, you may find that you have further questions about the reading. Please ring me on the telly tomorrow anytime to discuss whatever you wish."

By then, he'd have time to sort through it all. "Doc, I truly feel grateful for the opportunity to meet you. Rachel spoke so highly of you and I am glad we were able to get together."

"Thank you for sharing your time with me. The pleasure has been mine. I do so hope I have helped you in some small way."

"Well for starters, you helped me get over my fear of cats!" Getty jumped up and scurried out of the room, as if on cue.

The time they spent with Doc had flown by and he couldn't believe it had been over two hours since they walked in his front door. They all stood up and Rachel walked over to her old friend and wrapped her arms around Doc's neck. "Thank you."

Tommy reached out and shook his hand. "I look forward to my next leave and another meeting. Honestly, Doc, I feel as if I have a million questions, but I received a million answers today. I cannot express my gratitude enough." He reach into his pocket. "And how much for our readings today, sir?"

"That would be zero pounds."

Tommy laughed and Rachel gasped at Doc Cavanagh's generosity.

"No, sir. Seriously."

"Seriously. We'll see each other again. Until then, take this and you can pay me with it the next time we meet." He removed the amulet from his neck. The stone carving could almost be described as a human being in nearly a cross-like shape. "It symbolizes life. I would like you to have it."

"I couldn't."

"You can. You wouldn't want to offend an old man now, would you?"

"If I saw an old man I …"

"Tommy!" Rachel stopped him.

"Okay, okay! Thank you very much. I will wear it with hope and pride as a gift from a new friend. Thank you so much. It will be returned to you."

"Thomas, I hope you go on to consider what you have discovered during your reading."

Doc felt Rachel's emotional heaviness. She saw his smile, but his eyes were sad as she nodded, sharing an unspoken, silent farewell to her friend.

Chapter 11

As soon as he walked outside into the setting sun, Tommy took a deep breath and grasped Rachel's hand. Air deeply filled his lungs as he stood still. He looked up toward the sky, watching some wispy clouds create a light frosting of orange from the setting sun. His mind was caught up in the sorting of information from the last few hours.

Rachel watched him pensively and finally asked, "Are you okay, my love?"

Letting his breath out slowly, he nodded his head yes, but couldn't speak. His eyes filled with tears that he didn't let spill over his cheeks. He took one more soothing breath and smiled at her. "I need a drink."

"Then your wish is my command, sire!" Pulling on his arm to get him moving, she said, "Look, we'll go right across the street to Newman Arms."

Tommy laughed out loud. "Did Doc pick this location for moments like this when a client needs a drink?"

"You're daft!" She giggled. "The pub is almost two hundred years old. Let's get ourselves a well-deserved bevvy."

Walking inside Tommy admired the dark cherry wainscoting that lined the walls from floor to ceiling, further diminishing the brightness of the outside world since all the windows were covered due to the blackout.

A late afternoon crowd of workers had already filed into the pub for their social hour and a few pints. The sound of the radio news blurred under the sea of noise from the patrons laughing, talking and arguing. The bar, which extended the length of the room, had groups of people who periodically cheered about war news or an announcement about the availability of eggs.

It was a long narrow tavern with a staircase that led to the second floor for intimate dining or conversation. The hostess led them up the wrought iron staircase which gave Tommy an overview of the first floor of the pub. They took their seats at a corner table and ordered from a young waitress two pints plus two double vodka tonics.

He reached across the table to hold her hand. "I love you, Rach. I'm on overload. How about you?"

"I love you too, my fly-boy. I'm emotionally drained as well."

The waitress delivered their refreshments as they sat back and attempted to make sense of their unspoken thoughts. The radio was indiscernible on the second floor. The noise in the pub below was reminiscent of her pub, the air was filled with laughter, talking, and clanging of dishes.

She watched her Tommy sipping his vodka quietly. She knew he was in deep thought. "Tommy, what are you thinking about?"

He couldn't get Doc's story about Ellie from his head. He was glad that he'd met Roland Cavanagh. And Aunt Marilyn! He pondered the chance meeting of someone who lived in Baraboo, who also knew Doc. *The Nile River…? Why do I feel drawn to distinctive thoughts of Egypt?*

After ten minutes or so Rachel offered up a toast. "To Doc and your first reading."

"Yes, to Doc." He absentmindedly responded as if on autopilot. Would he and Rachel be doomed, like Doc and his Ellie? "And to *you* for twisting my arm to go see him. Thank you."

He looked at Rachel while toasting, his mind trying to fit answers together.

Suddenly Rachel smacked the table next to his glass and said in a loud, impatient voice, "So Thomas, tell me!" People at the next table stopped talking momentarily and stared at them. "I'm sitting right here, you know."

He had been drifting on the Nile. "Tell you what?"

"What the bloody hell are you thinking about? You mind letting me in on it? I know you like Doc, but what did you think of your reading? My reading? Anything?"

Attempting to gather himself he refocused and remembered his promise to Doc about Ellie…*Fuck*. Secrets. He shifted his mind from the past to the moment. "Sorry, Rach. I was thinking that he was spot on and it frightened me."

"Which part?"

He saw the concerned look on her face but he didn't want to betray Doc's trust.

Shuffling to stay present he said, "I'm not sure." He knew she could see he was scrambling. "But I do feel enlightened at the same time. Probably because you were with me. I couldn't and *wouldn't* have done that with anyone else, Rachel."

She knew he was lying about something, probably to protect her from some dark thoughts… *God, I love him so!*

She did them both a favor and changed the subject. "The amulet looks good on you."

"I still can't believe he gave it to me and wouldn't accept payment! I almost feel guilty. Hey, wait, did you pay him in advance?" She felt he was back in the here and now.

"No, no! Maybe it doesn't happen that often where you come from, but he's a good friend and a generous man. He has done that for me a few times over the last decade or so."

He smiled at her. "Oh, so you're my good luck charm. It wasn't my charming personality but the pretty girl on my arm."

"Tread lightly, fly-boy." She wouldn't allow herself to bite on his comment. Leaning forward she looked at him and said softly, "Can we talk about your AWOL comment?"

"What is there to talk about?" He spoke sharply as if trying to hold back his angst from her question.

She continued leaning toward him while talking softly, "What is there—buggers, Tommy! As splendid as that sounds, the fact is it won't work. I had no idea that you were entertaining thoughts like that. I can't wait to *not* be kissing you farewell until your next leave, however. Don't get me wrong—but I fear we would be haunted in the future." She inched away from him. "You only have five missions left. Finish them and we'll be free to be together with no ties to the war."

"And if I die before I complete my last mission? I looked around the city today and I saw the destruction of the bombs… hell yes, I'm mad at the war, but I'm doing the same thing in another city somewhere. I am a *fucking* hypocrite! Only I have *permission* to kill." His jaw tightened as he gritted his teeth.

She grabbed one of his white-knuckled, clenched fists curled on the table and Doc's warning about Tommy's temper came to mind.

"You are no-"

He held his hand up. "Stop, Rach. Please. I'm fine, really." He slammed back his vodka and Rachel sank back into her seat glad that the line of communication was finally open—even if it was uncomfortable.

Tommy wanted her to understand why he thought about going AWOL. She wanted to know too. After a few minutes of silence, he spoke. "One of my cards was the Empress–something about the harvest being here… entering a cycle of abundance, happiness and joy. But it was blocked, Rach! What if I never get to reap the rewards of the harvest? You!"

He reached across the table, urgently taking her hand into his. "I've waited my whole life to find you, my soul mate, but the fact the card is blocked scares the hell out of me." His eyes glistened with moisture as he hailed the waitress and ordered another vodka tonic.

Rachel's eyes also welled. *I can't lose him.* She wiped her tears away. "Maybe it wasn't a good idea to do the readings. I thought we would find more happiness and comfort in it."

She felt she needed a knife to cut through the thick emotional imbalance between them.

Tommy saw the anguish on Rachel's face and it rocked him emotionally to the core.

"You can't think like that." He gently squeezed her tender hand. He'd brought her down with his mood and regretted it. Tommy decided to make their last days light instead of dark. "But don't you see? All we need to do is figure out how to unblock what is already there." He mustered a look of hope.

Rachel's gaze remained clouded.

"I'm sorry, I didn't mean to upset you, my love." He leaned over and planted a kiss on her lips. "Let's continue enjoying our time together. Would you like to order something to eat?"

"I would prefer that, since it will be late when we get back home." Rachel spoke quietly.

Tommy looked over the menu and forced a smile. "I think I'll have the steak and kidney bean pie."

Much later they left the Newman Arms with the sliver of the moon shining above. It was a warm summer evening and they'd decided to walk since they had the time to get to Kings Cross Station and catch the train back.

Tommy stopped suddenly and lifted Rachel up, leaving her feet dangling a few feet from the ground as he embraced her.

He whispered into her ear, "I'm not sorry we went to see the Doc. He only shed light on things that we needed to know... un-muddied the waters, so to speak. As you said earlier, let's enjoy the rest of our time together. I love you, Rachel Smythe."

"I love you, Thomas Smith."

Right there, on the dimly moonlit street, they shared a long, intimate kiss; a kiss that lovers often share in private. Neither one of them wanted to come up for air as the moment was too sweet. Sad, but sweet and tender.

Chapter 12

Rachel spread a blanket on the floor in front of the fireplace and looked up at Tommy, standing by the loveseat. "Darling, could you pour me a whiskey, please?"

"Yes, my love." An anguished expression crossed her face as she scribbled in her journal. He delivered the whiskey to where she sat on the blanket. Her blue-green eyes appeared troubled. "Is something wrong?"

"Tommy, time is going by so bloody quickly! I can't believe it's Friday night already. I feel like you just kissed me hello at the pub. Tomorrow night will be here before we know it."

He sat down next to her on the blanket. "Time flies when you're having fun," Tommy kissed her neck hoping to break her downward spiral of emotions.

A single tear rolled down her cheek while she looked up at him. "I apologize for being so emotional—we Brits aren't known for displaying our emotions very easily, but you've changed me…"

Putting his arms around her, he softly laid his head on her shoulder. "I like you this way… just the way you are," he whispered in her ear.

"But we need to stop it!" she retorted harshly.

Just the thought of losing her made his heart race. His mind shifted gears while the fear encompassed his being. *I knew this was coming. Our relationship was always too good to be true. Today was too much for her to handle, I'm a soldier and it could be over.* He slowly backed away from her.

She interrupted his thought process as she caressed his face. "Time, love! I meant we need to stop Father Time." Her voice trembled as she pulled him back into her arms.

"Oh! I'll drink to that. TIME STAND STILL!" he shouted.

They clinked glasses and sipped to time standing still.

He returned to her delicate neck as his heartbeat sped up with the taste of her skin. Tracing with his tongue a path up to the tender spot just beneath her earlobe sent chills down her body.

She wanted to fight the immediate urge to stop him, thinking somehow it would slow time down, but she couldn't–it felt too good to have him touching her with such sensual tenderness.

"Can we stop it?" she said softly.

Again, he backed away from her. "Be clear what you're telling me to stop, Rach. You're confusing me here."

"Time. Can we stop time?"

"So, you're not telling me to stop kissing you. Good. Because I don't want to stop. The train ride seemed to take forever. All I could think about was you and this moment." *Does she understand my need to be one with her body?*

"And now it's here. You're right. Time does fly when you're having fun." She leaned into him, pulling her hair to one side, exposing the rest of her neck.

"Time flies when you desperately want to live and breathe every moment you have with the one you want to spend an eternity with." He leaned over and sucked on her neck, leaving a hickey.

Rachel felt her body give into him. She didn't care if she had to wear a scarf for a month until his love mark faded, it felt too good to stop him.

"More. More, please." She grabbed his hair.

"My pleasure." Tommy pulled off her pants and the emerald green fabric floated to the floor, she unbuttoned her blouse. Kissing her belly, just below her navel—wanting to taste the sweetness between her legs had his mouth watering. Again she shivered from the pleasure of his tongue.

He began to tongue her belly button which drove her hips upward toward his mouth. Their hands met while reaching for her panties at the same time, each pulling one side down until they were no longer touching her toes.

There she lay on the blanket with just her bra on in front of the fire.

"You're so beautiful, Rach. How did I get so lucky?"

"You're about to get really lucky, my fly-boy. But here," she flipped over, exposing her naked backside, "take off this uncomfortable bra, please."

Tommy leaned over her and ran his tongue from her ass all the way to the back of her bra, then he unsnapped it. She leaned on her bent elbows and once released, she tossed her bra aside. She started to flip back over, but he stopped her.

Instinctually she raised her hips higher in the air as one of his hands began to gently spread apart the glistening lips between her legs from behind. She was already dripping wet with desire for him and his fingers slid inside her easily.

She moaned with sheer pleasure, "Oh, baby… That feels so good..."

He gently thrust his fingers deeper, massaging her slick walls as she hummed, "Uh-hummmm… oh, baby, that's perfect." He felt his fingers being swallowed by her pussy walls as she began to climb toward an orgasm. "Yes, yes. Please, don't stop…" she cried as she was grinding her clit deeply into his palm.

Tommy followed her needy and breathy instructions and within moments she was gasping for air as she had her orgasm. He was licking between her ass cheeks as her body shuddered with orgasmic intensity.

"My goodness… I love what you do to me..." She slowly regained her breath and he gently withdrew his fingers which had her tasty wetness on them.

He slid one finger into his mouth and then the other into her mouth. She quickly flipped over and grabbed at his head to pull him in for a deep kiss, sharing the taste of her orgasm.

"More, please." She whispered sensuously in his ear and Tommy dipped down between her legs. He mouthed her pulsating clit while her body shuddered with mini aftershocks.

"I need more. More, meaning you inside me!"

Tommy pulled his pants off as Rachel ripped open his shirt exposing his perfectly chiseled chest and abdomen. He climbed on top of her and slid inside her. She wrapped her legs around the small of his back and pulled him in deeper with her feet locked on his ass. Her hands pulled at his thick black hair as she brought her mouth to one of his nipples and gently bit it while her tongue swirled around the tip of it.

Their lovemaking was perfectly in sync. Thrust after thrust.

He started to feel her wet walls clamp around his slickened, thick cock. Calling out each other's name, they came simultaneously with the crackling of the fire as their only light.

"You're my perfect match. My soul mate." She whispered as he groaned and kissed her ear… right where he'd started the night.

"You're my one great love," Tommy added.

They enjoyed being in front of the fire, both completely exposed to each other. Finishing their drinks, Tommy offered to bathe her, to which she acquiesced.

After their soothing bath, they were physically and mentally exhausted and made their way to the bedroom where they passed out after blowing out the candles on the nightstand.

Chapter 13

August 12, 1944, 7:24 a.m.

In the early light of dawn on Saturday morning Tommy had woken to the sound of a B-17 taking off in the distance, knowing they must be going on a mission deep into Germany. He made coffee and sat at the bay window, admiring all the colors of the flowers in the garden.

His mind sorted through yesterday's visit with Doc Cavanaugh as he touched the amulet adorning his neck, wondering how long ago it had been made. The cards had not given him an answer to his immediate desire of finishing his tour of duty and living out his life with Rachel. *All they told me was how I needed to do the right thing. Doc is still looking for Ellie on the other side yet he appears to be fulfilled without her.*

Fuck! What if my blocks are telling me Rachel will die and I will need to wait for her? His mind struggled to grasp how not to lose hope. *In truth, love is so delicate. While my search is controlled by each breath I take and each beat of my heart, I know there is more than the moment. All I can do in the now is to choose the right thing, and be in the hands of the …*

The creak of the wooden floor startled him and he turned around. "Good morning, sunshine."

Rachel wore her favorite soft pink cotton robe and held a cup of hot tea. "Good morning, fly-boy."

"Sorry, Rach. I didn't even hear you come out and go to the kitchen. I would have brought you your tea in bed, my love."

Rachel joined him on the bay window bench snuggling her back against his bare chest. "I didn't want to interrupt you. You had that faraway look and I wanted you to have your time." Rubbing her face against his neck, she sweetly kissed his skin.

He lifted her head up so that he could look into her radiant green eyes. "I am so in love with you. Here I sit with you, the sun rising over my shoulder, the flowers in full bloom. I'm surrounded by beauty wherever I turn. Tell me this is real. Because if it's a dream, don't wake me."

Rachel just smiled at him.

Leaning forward he placed his lips on hers joining together their two souls, making one heart and mind as they melded into each other.

"Yes, my long lost love, it's real." Rachel sighed. "But promise me, Thomas, that it is forever. Not just in this lifetime, but for always and all ways. You must find me each lifetime no matter how deeply we find ourselves twisted in time."

"Promise! But you must promise me as well." He slid his hands into her robe bringing them up to her full breasts. Rachel grabbed his wrists, pulling his hands away.

"Listen up fly-boy, we'll get around to that. I have today all planned out."

He loved her sassy personality. "Oh, really?" He grinned while wondering what she had in mind.

"Yes. The first thing we are going to do is plant a seedling I bought at the farmer's market. We are going to watch it grow so big that one day we'll be able to sit under it when we're old and gray... It's a Rowan, they live for over two hundred years. The tree will live long enough for our great-great grandchildren to play under it when we're long gone."

She hopped up, grabbing his empty coffee cup and strutted off to the kitchen. He watched her beautiful ass swaying back and forth as she disappeared.

"How about some breakfast first?"

"No problem, fly-boy." She returned moments later with his coffee and a plate of warmed crumb cake which she placed on the window bench next to him.

"Thank you." He thought of how badly he wanted to grow old with her.

She laughed at his expression. "Yes, to whatever is going on in that head of yours, but *after* we plant the tree. Then we'll have a picnic. So wake up, farm boy, drink your coffee and after you've eaten, I suggest you get the shovel from the shed while I pack the picnic basket."

"Yes, ma'am!" He mock saluted her. "Did you pick the spot for the seedling?"

"I thought we would do that together."

Taking another mouthful of crumb cake he felt detached from the moment as if he was out of his body and watching from above.

⟡

Tommy leaned on the shovel in the yard, taking a break after beginning the hole. He was staring at the cottage when something in the window caught his attention. Two people stood inside looking out the bay window. Trying to be friendly, he waved, but they had already turned their backs to him.

He had almost thought the woman was Rachel but she had on a winter overcoat. He went back to digging, thinking Rachel would bring her friends out to meet him.

A little later, Tommy smelled the cookies Rachel was baking on the breeze as he headed back to the cottage to get a drink of water.

He walked into the kitchen. "Is that Aunt Marilyn's recipe that I smell?"

"That depends." Wiping her hands on her apron and putting her hands on her hips. "Is that tree in the ground already?"

"I only have to stake it up."

"Then your answer is no, you're not finished?" She crossed her arms over her flour-covered apron.

"Well, you didn't ask if I was finished."

"Okay, smartass. It's almost eleven. Hurry up! I'm getting hungry."

"No kidding, Miss Grumpy Pants."

"Pardon?" She adjusted a loose hair that had fallen from her bun.

"Nothing, m'lady. Say, who were those people that came by?" He went to the sink and refilled his water glass.

"What people?" Rachel turned from the stove. "When?"

"Just a little while ago. I saw a couple looking in my direction. They were standing in front of the bay window, right there." He pointed.

"Oh, my. That high altitude sickness just won't go away," she teased him.

"No, Rach, really. I *saw* them. The lady almost looked like you from a distance, but she was wearing a winter overcoat."

"Heatstroke then?" She put her hand on his forehead with a giggle.

"No! Come on, don't tease me. I know what I saw." He felt stupid for a moment as he swallowed the water still looking at her, but he knew he hadn't imagined the couple being there.

"Well, my love, no one was here. I would have known if they were. Stop procrastinating, fly-boy."

They stared at one another then suddenly Rachel's eyes lit up, "Tommy, you must have had one of your visions. That's the only logical explanation. Nobody has been in the house with me."

"Hmm, perhaps you're right. I was just staring at the cottage, taking a break. Wonder who they were… why it was revealed to me… maybe I'll call Doc later. I do have a few questions for him that I thought of." He placed his glass in the sink and slapped her ass as he walked by.

"HEY, you!" she squealed while she rubbed her ass cheek. "He meant it, so take him up on his offer. And by the way, I'm not grumpy, I'm needy. And you're in no condition to give me what I *need* at the moment."

"What would that be?" He returned to wrap his mud-covered hands around her waist.

"You, bathed and naked."

She grabbed a large wooden spoon from the drawer.

"You just want me for my body." Tommy backed away as if she was going to hit him.

"That's right, fly-boy. I just want you for your perfect body. And not your mind. Hurry up, or you'll be wishing you did when I go to find a different guy for the job."

"Yes, ma'am."

Tommy hurried off to finish his tree duties and once finished, he jumped in the bath. Rachel finished packing the picnic basket. She quickly undressed herself while Tommy was still in the bathroom and laid naked on the bed, waiting for him.

He walked out of the bath with a towel around his waist. Rachel was lounging naked on top of the comforter and slid off the bed and ripped the towel away. She began to lick and suck him until he nearly came in her mouth.

"Now… I want you inside of me… now!"

"My pleasure!" His cock was aching to be inside her.

They shared more than lovemaking–this time it was primal sex. They needed each other's bodies desperately. Tommy and Rachel took turns being pleased and pleasing the other until they were both completely satisfied.

"I thought we were going for a picnic?" he asked while lying naked on his side. He was waiting for her to return as she walked out of the bathroom.

"We are. Get dressed, fly-boy."

"I don't know if I can move."

"I bet you can!" She studied him as he rested against a pillow. "I have a few ideas about our picnic that would make you want to move…" she flashed a naughty smile in his direction while she got dressed.

Chapter 14

A small secluded area by a creek not far from home beckoned them.

"This is the spot I have been saving to share with you, my love," Rachel said. They spread a faded red and blue checkered blanket under the large, mature Rowan tree which provided a beautiful, welcomed umbrella from the hot rays of the sun. A few yards away from where they lay on the blanket, the sound of the waist-high creek's water bubbled on its journey to the large pond it fed. Tommy popped the cork on a bottle of chardonnay and poured two glasses, then came down next to her.

Rolling over onto his back next to her, he could see the early afternoon sky peeking through the leaves above, and fantasized that time had stopped as he held her hand. He brought her hand to his lips, planting a kiss on it. But when his lips joined her hand, a surge of energy between them overtook his mind's eye and placed him in a different place and time that he knew was well after the war. The time warp only lasted for a millisecond, but he clearly saw her in an emerald green dress with long sheer flowing sleeves, her hair in a wispy braid off her left shoulder while locking eyes with her from across a room. She walked toward him with a smile on her face and an outstretched hand.

Rachel was unaware of what he was thinking as she felt his lips touch her hand. "Did I tell you all the reasons why I picked the Rowan seedling to plant in our yard?"

He didn't respond. But the top of her hand was still on his lips so she continued.

"The Celtics called it the Wizard Tree. The Rowan was considered sacred by them."

When he didn't reply, Rachel pulled her hand away, rolling over on her side and sipped some of the wine from her glass. She looked at Tommy who was just lying on his back gazing into the sky. Filling her mouth with wine, she leaned over, placing her lips on his. She allowed the wine to trickle into his mouth from hers while looking into his eyes.

Just then she realized he wasn't there with her in the moment–he was drifting in the cosmos.

She stayed quiet, the sound of the birds filling the air, wishing she could be one with him. *God, time has stopped,* she thought, while admiring his beautiful facial features and gorgeous blue eyes. After a bit, he seemed to come back to reality.

"Where did you go, darling?"

"I did it again, didn't I?" His concern gave insight to his confusion.

"Yes, unless you were purposefully ignoring me." She chuckled.

"No, never. What were you saying… something about the tree?"

"I'm actually more interested in *where you were.*"

"Crazy. It's just so crazy that I hardly want to embarrass myself with telling you."

He looked at her and knew what her sweet, yet stern expression meant. "And no, I wasn't flying again. I saw another glimpse of you… in the future. The lifetime is not this one." His breath caught and he continued, "We meet again, Rach. I'm sure of it. And I recognize you from your eyes. That's how we'll always know each other in other lifetimes, by our eyes. The vision was so clear, as clearly as you sit here this very second." His body trembled.

Her breath hitched while her eyes welled with tears and goosebumps covered her exposed flesh.

"Don't be sad, my love. Please don't cry, unless they're happy tears." He begged.

"I don't know how I feel actually," as her tears rolled off her cheeks onto his face.

"Just know to look for me always and we'll find each other." He sat up and sighed, taking her into his embrace, shaking his head. "Doc's right about the future." He mumbled softly to himself, "He's waiting too."

"What does that mean?"

"I promised him I wouldn't tell anyone, including you. You can respect a gentleman's promise, can't you?"

"Of course. It's between you and Doc. But is he sad? I'd hate to think of him still waiting *and* sad."

"No, he's not sad. We'll just leave it at that, fair?"

"Fair enough. I love you, Thomas Phillip Smith."

"And I love you, Rachel Christie Smythe."

They shared a tender, loving kiss although neither closed their eyes as they gazed into the other's.

Suddenly Rachel jumped back a few inches and blurted out, "Do you realize that's twice in one day that you've been able to see the *future me?*"

"Dear Lord! You're right!" He took a deep breath. "I saw Doc just yesterday. Do you think that has anything to do with it? Perhaps yesterday we removed blocks and opened a window for me to see more clearly?"

"Bloody hell, I didn't even put it together! You're spot on! Tommy, I can only imagine what you'll conjure up for the rest of our lives as we continue to see him for readings and the like." Then she smiled widely, "However, just one question... am I pretty?"

"Of course, baby, you're beautiful!"

She beamed and kissed him again.

"One can only imagine what I'll see next." He agreed and looked away from her to study the tree. In his heart, he feared he wouldn't live as long as she would. It would possibly be a tragic ending–of which he wasn't sure, but that thought alone brought about angst he didn't want her to notice, so he smiled and changed the subject.

"Now then, back to the tree. What were you saying?"

She repeated what she'd said earlier, then added, "My mother was the one who interested me in its origin. She studied all types of atypical things. I even brought the book with me she made notes in."

Rachel pulled the book from the picnic basket and flipped through it. When she found the spot she was looking for, she handed it to him. He read it aloud.

"The Rowan tree, known as the Tree of Life, has scarlet red berries in summertime, like living drops of blood–proof to the ancestors of its life-force, it is believed to have mighty powers of protection. Rowan berry necklaces and Rowan loops were used as a charm or amulet. The wood of the Rowan was considered right only if collected from a living tree, after asking the Rowan's permission first, of course. Some believe fairies live in its branches, and play amidst springtime's white flowers. Stealing the wood at any time without their consent might focus their anger in your direction."

He closed the book and smiled at her. "You realize we met in springtime and now its summertime. Do you believe that fairies live in the branches?"

"Of course! Yet one must believe in fairies to begin with first. I believe in fairies! Do you?"

"I'm believing more and more that there is more to life than the eye can see. So yes, I guess I do believe in fairies."

She kissed him again and reached down and lifted her thin-strapped sundress over her head, exposing her naked body. "Dearest fairies, please look the other way because I'm not asking for permission for what I'm about to do next..."

The weather was unseasonably hot for mid-August in the English countryside. Sweat lightly covered Tommy's brow as Rachel sat astride his lap. He removed his shirt while she pulled his trousers down. He easily slid inside her.

A few droplets of sweat dripped onto his chest from her nipples as she sat up, leaning against his bent knees.

⋯≒◉◐≒⋯

After a few moments of basking in their sensual afterglow, they decided a dip in the secluded pond was necessary.

They were lying naked while air drying on the blanket when Rachel said, "Our time is going by so quickly—baby, it's already Saturday afternoon. I wish I could stop the hands of time." Her eyes suddenly filled with tears.

"Oh, baby. Don't cry. Just think, the faster the time goes, the sooner I will be back in your arms. Remember, only five missions left and then we can be together forever."

"Forever? You promise?"

He lay on top of her sliding his cock into her again. "Rachel Christie Smythe, I'm going to ask you to marry me one day soon."

"And you already know the answer… but I'll wait until you ask. I don't want you to think you have it made in the shade." She giggled and kissed him as she felt his erection stiffening deeply inside her. She gently grinded her hips, stirring his desire again and they made slow, passionate, all-consuming love this time.

⋯≒◉◐≒⋯

Tommy walked up to Rachel and crouched behind her. She was sitting bare-skinned on one of the large, smooth rocks in the creek with her feet dangling in the water.

"I'm sorry I don't have a ring yet, but how about this as a promise ring? Will it do for now?"

He placed on her finger a circle of woven Rowan wood with a berry he'd asked the fairies if it was okay to take from their tree.

"It's perfect, my fly-boy."

"I love you, my sassy Brit."

She smiled and turned to wrap around him. They lost their balance and fell into the creek naked.

A few hours later, after they dried in the warmth of the sun, she unpacked the rest of the food while he sat on a rock sunning himself. Standing up to make sure she liked the way the spread looked she said, "I have prepared a standard English picnic fare for you, Lieutenant. Deviled eggs, Cornish pasty, and custard tarts. Hope it's to your liking." Rachel turned to see him staring up at the sky. "Tommy!" Her hands were on her hips. "Thomas Smith, where's your head? You're not a fly-boy today; you're on leave! Can you please stop getting lost in the sky? Today, you're all mine! I made you your favorite lunch."

He was enjoying the moment and not even thinking of the war, recalling their unabashed outdoor lovemaking they had throughout the day. "What was that, baby?"

"Your lunch! It's a Spam sandwich, of course! Mustard or mayo?" She giggled. "Come on, my sweet Tommy. We don't have much time left before your leave is over." She wrapped her arms around him. "Let's pretend the bloody war is done and we're just a young couple in love having a risqué afternoon in the countryside, agreed?"

"Agreed! Then let's not bring up the war. I'm not a pilot right now… I'm a lover." He stared into her face, memorizing every line around her eyes while she smiled at him, the shape of her full lips. Her vibrant green eyes were filled with love and desire for him, her chestnut hair was pulled off to one side. The birds were singing, flowers bloomed, it was perfect. And yet, he looked back up into the blue, cloudless sky at the sound of a distant aircraft engine, which only sullied the moment of pure bliss—he still was an active member of the war.

"Tommy, will you stop thinking about being a B-17 pilot?" Rachel frowned. "Don't leave me, my love. I love you so much, words cannot describe. So be with me and spend the rest of today enveloped in us before I go crazy and really make you eat a Spam sandwich!"

"You wouldn't." He crouched with his hands on the ready for a serious tickling session, which she always attempted, but failed, to fight off.

"I'm tempted! Now that we're engaged to be engaged, you're mine and I'm yours. I wish this was your last mission and then we could be pre-planning the engagement party. Wait 'til I tell Izzy!"

"Let's eat, love, I'm starving."

The sun was a few hours from setting on Saturday, what would be their last full day together before his leave was over. They were still under the Rowan tree, wrapped in each other's embrace enjoying the peace and beauty of the day they shared.

"I'm sorry to say, but it's time to wrap up our day here and begin our evening at home. Are you ready to head back to the cottage?" Rachel asked.

"Sure thing, then I can call Doc." Tommy knelt down and packed the picnic basket as Rachel folded the blanket.

They walked in silence, holding hands to the cottage—both lost in thought. Tommy was thrilled that Rachel had agreed to be his wife, although he didn't know if he'd live long enough to actualize their dream of being husband and wife; Rachel was reliving the moment when they toppled into the stream after he asked to be engaged to her with the sweetest handmade ring imaginable.

Once inside, Tommy lit a fire as the night air was cool again and poured a whiskey while Rachel bathed. They were already in a couple's easy synchronicity.

Their relationship was deeper than either had ever experienced before, although both were engaged to other people in the past. Rachel's fiancé had died in the war and Tommy's fiancée had left him after his first training accident back in the States.

Looking back upon those relationships, they seemed trite to what they shared now with each other.

Before Rachel finished her bath, Tommy took the opportunity to call Doc Cavanagh. He answered on the third ring.

"Doc Cavanagh, Tommy Smith here."

"Thomas, my fine young bloke. I'm so pleased you rang. I suppose you have a few hundred questions for me?" The older man chuckled.

"Yes, yes I do. Mainly, how do I unblock the Empress before I leave on my next mission?"

"I'm not sure how to unblock the card itself. Each person's path has its own winding road."

"Then let's put it this way—I'm not afraid of dying, but I'm angry with the thought of dying before I reap the rewards of the harvest she represents." His voice shook with frustration.

"First of all, you'll need to remain calm, Thomas. You're measuring your happiness only by a lifetime, by what you have in the present. Open your mind and allow yourself to see. How do you know it doesn't represent future happiness in another life? Stop trying to control the outcome, and cease to live in just this moment."

"But, Doc, I want THIS harvest, not the next one! I want Rachel, Doc. We belong together!"

"The cards speak the truth, Thomas, whether we like it or not. Do you fear that Rachel will only exist in this life?"

"No, but I suppose you can call me greedy for wanting it all. I'm positive I have seen a flash or two of her in the future."

"First let me ask you, how did you know it was Rachel in the future?"

"As soon as I looked into her eyes, I knew."

"Then you should enjoy the journey, the path upon which you travel, and stop trying to control it. You can't."

Tommy was silent for a few moments, reflecting on what Doc just said. He was convinced there was no way of changing the future he already knew was looming.

"Thomas? Are you still there?"

"Yes, Doc, I'm here." He spoke sadly, sinking down in the loveseat, watching the fire crackle.

"I surmise you do not like the answers I've given you tonight. But keep in mind this is not your first lifetime, nor will it be your last. Your soul is on a journey encased in *this* body. And it will journey for as long as it chooses to. All I can advise you to do is be happy with what you've been gifted by the Masters thus far."

"Thank you, Doc. I'll try."

"Godspeed, son."

Click.

Chapter 15

Tommy finished his bath while Rachel heated up the mutton stew that she had prepared earlier in the day. She looked in the mirror in the foyer at her hair and makeup, making sure it was to her liking in her quest to look pretty for him. She placed her long braid on the front of her left shoulder. She again dressed in the new outfit he'd treated her to the day before, along with her brown ankle boots.

Rachel scrutinized the table setting, making sure everything was in place. She lit the candles and poured two glasses of wine. "Perfect," she said softly then turned off the house lights.

Tommy picked up the aroma as he entered the room. "God, sweetheart, that smells good!"

His eyes adjusted to the candlelight and he saw her standing there—he stopped in his tracks while catching his breath at how beautiful she looked.

She spun around for him like a model she had seen in London at a charity fashion show.

"I'm sorry, Miss, if I seem confused. I was supposed to meet a hot, cute barmaid that I proposed to earlier today. But all I see before me is a beautiful goddess."

Rachel started to giggle. "Cute, fly-boy. God, I love you. Wine, my love?" Holding the glass he saw the dancing candlelight aglow in her eyes.

He set the two glasses down and pulled her into his body for a passionate embrace, he ran his big hands down her back and cupped her ass. "Sweetheart, you look and feel beautiful." They shared a long, sensual kiss as their tongues played with the other, breathing in each other's breath.

After a few moments, he slowly backed away from her even though he wanted to undress her and be inside her body. "I want to store this vision of you in my brain."

"Well, I understand how you feel…looking at you." She began to snicker as she walked away.

"Oh, that's funny to you?" he asked, checking his zipper to make sure it was up.

She nodded her head yes as she continued toward the kitchen still giggling.

He picked up the wine and took a mouthful. "So, what's so funny? You want to let me in on the secret?"

"Perhaps you need to look in the mirror." She returned from the kitchen carrying the stew and dinner rolls for the table.

She watched Tommy look in the mirror where she saw him smile at his bright red lips and he joined in her laughter. *This is how I want to remember my soul mate until he returns to me… His laughter that fills the air, he's so full of life.*

"What? You don't like the color?" They laughed harder.

She was dishing up his stew as she watched him wiping his lips on the napkin. *God I want him to always be with me.* It began to sink in that this could be their last meal together in this lifetime.

"I want to thank you for the most beautiful few days of my life, Rachel. I want to marry you when I return on my next leave. I can't wait any longer. If I wasn't leaving in the morning, we'd be running to the Chaplin."

She could only nod her head yes as tears began to stream down her face smearing her mascara onto her cheeks. "Oh, my sweet Tommy, yes." Both barely ate anything despite the fact of how good it tasted.

She broke into full blown tears and dropped her fork. "I'm sorry, Tommy, for falling apart in front of you." She sobbed. "I love you so much and I know I need to be strong for you!" Suddenly she tossed her napkin aside while pushing her chair back so hard it tipped over as she ran from the table to the bedroom.

Tommy followed her into the bedroom, stopping at the doorway. Rachel was curled up in a fetal position on the bed and crying hysterically. He didn't know what to do or say. It broke his heart to watch her fall apart because of him.

Needing to compose himself he turned away from her to wipe the tears of frustration that had already filled his eyes. *Oh, my God. How could my beautiful love for her do this to her?* His body stiffened with anger for he knew how powerless he was to change the most likely outcome.

Walking back into the living room he poured them two whiskies, hoping it would help her calm down. When he returned to bedroom, she was still lying on the bed in the same position. Placing the whiskey on the nightstand, he laid down next to her pulling her gently into his arms, and he began to rock her.

"I could go AWOL and I would for you, Rach."

Her sobbing deepened and he knew that was the wrong string of words for the emotional moment. The right words finally came to him: "Sweetheart, you're not letting me down."

"But, I, I, I should be stronger for you."

"You're exactly who you are supposed to be. Do you think I want to marry a robot? You're sweet, sensitive, sassy, loving and sexy. Rach, baby, you're my match. Right after we first met, I wrote a sonnet for you. Would you like to hear it, my love?" He held her, still rocking her. Breaking free of his arms she sat up and looked at him.

"You wrote a poem for me?"

"Yes, it's not great but it is from my heart." It put a small smile on her face. "I poured you a whiskey to help you get through the reading." He chuckled.

"No one's ever written a sonnet for me before. I'm certain it's perfect."

Tommy was glad to see her composure returning. "Well, don't laugh, but being the pilot on a plane gives me the right to make my crew listen to whatever I want to say to them. So, for the last fifteen missions I've read them my poem and they all hated it." He waited for her reaction.

She giggled at the thought of what he just told her. "You didn't do that, but is the poem real?"

"Yes, may I read it to you? However, I suggest we both finish our whiskey." They clinked their glasses and tossed them back. Moving to the edge of the bed he pulled it out of his pants pocket and unfolded it. He cleared his throat.

A Lost Romance Found
by Thomas P. Smith. May 21, 1944

The touch of your lips upon mine cause my heart to pause.
Your skin so soft,
The taste of your lips,
The smell of your hair,
The green of your eyes,
Is this just another dream from long ago?
For who am I? But a drop of rain upon a sea.
And as my heart begins to beat I feel it is in unison with
yours now
as we become one in mind and soul.
I know how long in time I've been searching for this
moment, my love,
for you and it will never die.
And you will always be my brightest star on the darkness
night
'Til I'm home in your arms once more.

He sat there looking at the paper and waited for her response.

Suddenly her arms were around his neck as she pulled him on top of her and back onto the bed. "Can I see it my fly-boy?"

Grabbing the paper from his hand they laid there intertwined while she reread every word. He stroked every part of her body that he could reach. The fabric she was wearing was thin enough that he could almost feel her skin.

Neatly refolding the paper, she released herself from his embrace and got out of bed. "Thank you, my love, for every word you wrote. It will be treasured forever. Now I have a treat for you, my poet. So, sit back and relax."

"May I freshen our whiskies?" He wasn't sure what to expect but was glad she was at least feeling better. Pouring the two whiskies he heard the Harry James orchestra playing "Skylark" as he walked back to the bedroom. He handed her the drink, which she placed on the dresser, and he sat back down on the edge of the bed.

"To us till the end of time." Tommy took a sip as she began to sway back and forth to the rhythm of the music.

She stood at the doorway and seductively stripped away her clothing, starting with her pants. She undid the button and zipper allowing it to slide to the floor, revealing her sexy panties and the beauty of her shapely legs. Turning around she continued to sway while leaning forward so he could admire her silk-covered ass while she unbuttoned her top, slowly sliding it off her shoulders, then down her back and finally letting the green silk fall to floor.

Still with her back to him she reached around and unsnapped her bra, sliding it off. At last, she slid her panties off revealing her bare, beautiful white ass to him as she continued to sway to the music with her chestnut hair kissing her mid-back.

Rachel slowly turned around to face him while pinching her full, erect nipples, her mouth slightly open. Once the music ended, she stood waiting for him. Tommy jumped up from the bed dropping to his knees wanting to lick her when she pulled him back up to a standing position. "Look at me, my sweet Tommy." She cupped his face with her hands. "Look into my eyes and hold onto what you see until you come home to me. And yes, I will marry you when you return. Yet, it doesn't matter if we are married or not for I am *yours* until the end of time, darling. Do you understand that? *Yours.*"

His gaze locked with her vibrant greenish-blue eyes which were filled with love. He could almost see the glow of her aura as he tried to capture and record everything about her face deep into his mind's eye.

Tommy pulled her into a passionate kiss as the taste of her mouth filled his. Her body and the scent of her hair and skin were intoxicating.

"You're so beautiful, Rachel. Every time I see you, I fall even more in love with you, the you that is inside here," he pointed to her heart and then her forehead, "that only I can see."

"I need you inside of me. Let's make love now."

She slithered against him, unzipped his pants and pulled out his hard cock. She swallowed his size as far as she could. He fell back and melded into the bed, surrendering to her tantalizing tongue, lips and hands.

Feeling her mouth devour him, he watched her bare back and ass as long as he could before exploding into her mouth. He pulled her up to his face. She still had some of his semen running down her chin and he licked her lips to taste himself. He shed his remaining clothes, not sure who tore off what, and climbed on top of her.

⋅⋗⎯⎯◉⎯⎯⋖⋅

A short time later, Tommy was awoken by a kiss on the back of his neck and he slowly rolled over. Rachel climbed on top of him and bit his left nipple. Hard. Very hard. She suckled his flesh and didn't release her bite for what seemed like forever.

"Ouch, baby! What's this for? Was I a bad boy or something?" Tommy rubbed his chest, smiling while looking at a teeth-shaped indentation on his skin around his nipple which was already changing into a deep purple.

"Just wanted to brand you. So if any other woman sees it on your bare chest she will know you belong to me." She tapped her own chest.

"Rachel, we are already married in my heart and soul."

"Oh, my sweet Tommy. How you own my heart."
She gently sobbed.

"I'm so in love with you, my sassy Brit." He softly
caressed her face with his fingertips.

"Tommy, make love to me, please."

⋆⇒◉⇐⋆

Rachel was curled up into his arms with her head resting on
his bare chest. "Tommy, there's something I need to speak
with you about."

"What is it, baby?" He let the scent of her hair fill his
head.

"You know how you have been able to see things
before they happen?" *God, give me the strength,* she
thought, almost afraid to say what she was thinking.

"Yes…" he pensively replied.

Lifting her cheek off his chest to look into his face, she
spoke barely above a whisper, "Please don't fly tomorrow. I
have a bad feeling about it."

He exhaled deeply.

"I always have a bad feeling before each mission and
most of the guys do. My crew needs me and unless I'm
physically unfit I must be there."

He tried to reassure her that everything would be just
fine. She was not convinced, nor was he.

August 13, 1944 - 2 a.m.

They fell back asleep but Tommy woke an hour later. It always happened the night before a mission. Preflight jitters he called it.

In addition, the fact that the love of his life asked him not to fly this specific mission was weighing heavily on his mind for two reasons: First, she never asked him not to fly; and secondly, he knew she was right, but he had already decided the life of his crew was in his hands.

He knew he should fall back to sleep, but he lay there with his mind running wild with thoughts of Rachel and the past few days they'd spent together, the visions of the future, even the day they met.

Tommy got up and went to the bay window where he grabbed Rachel's journal from the old cigar box she kept it in. He ripped out a page and scribbled a note to her.

My Darling Rachel, I want you to have this. Hold onto it until I return for you. Hopefully it won't be that long. I love you more than mere words could ever express. I hope you know this. Always and all ways, your sweet Tommy.

He neatly folded the paper with the amulet that Doc gave him inside the paper and placed it under her journal inside the cigar box.

Reliving almost every detail of their night, Tommy stood in the kitchen, drinking a glass of tap water. He looked out the window at their garden of vibrant flowers.

Suddenly, Rachel slipped her arms around him from behind, pulling her naked body tightly against him. "Come lay with me until you leave."

She took his hand and led him back to the bedroom.

An hour and a half later, Tommy was in uniform standing in front of the full-length beveled floor mirror. Rachel came up from behind him wearing her bathrobe, holding a hot cup of coffee for him. Her hair was perfectly tousled from their night of lovemaking and intense sex.

"Hi, beautiful," he whispered.

"Hi, handsome," she whispered back.

They only wanted to say positive things to each other, just like every time he left for a mission since they'd fallen in love back in May.

"I cannot help but wonder why it seems a little different this time, Tommy. Any clue?"

"Maybe because we're engaged now." He smacked her ass gently.

"Right, right. That makes sense, I suppose."

"And we'll marry as soon as I get back." But what he was really thinking was that he'd never told Rachel about *FiFi* needing to be repaired from his last mission.

He took the cup of coffee and placed it on the nightstand to pull her into his arms. "Rach, I love you. I'll be back as soon as I can. Remember only five missions left…"

"I know. But for now, just kiss me and promise me you'll come back for me."

"I'll always come back for you. It's your eyes. I can't live without those eyes looking back at me."

"These eyes will be waiting for you. Always and all ways."

"Always and all ways, Rach. We'll always know each other by our eyes." He smiled at her.

Just then the unwanted honk of the horn from the military bus sounded. He could hear Alex screaming, "Come on, Cap! Kiss her good-bye and get your ass out here!"

They stood still, looking at each other, both breathless.

"Get back into bed. I want to picture you naked in bed, okay my love?"

"Whatever you want. Just come back to me." She softly smiled.

"I'm yours, forever."

"Always?"

"And all ways. Rest my beautiful love. Rest now. I'll see you..."

They kissed sweetly, while Rachel held back her tears. She wanted to show him how strong she was while she awaited his return.

He walked away and stopped at the bedroom door. He turned to look at her one more time. She blew him a kiss and he pretended to catch it, put it in his pocket, right over the spot where she'd "branded" him.

Rachel watched him leave the bedroom and she sobbed, as she always did when he left for his missions. The front door closed and she heard the bus drive off with the love of her life, with her Tommy in it.

She threw her teacup against the wall and buried her face into his pillow so she could smell his essence and cried herself to sleep.

He jumped on the bus with less enthusiasm than he ever exhibited before. As they drove off, he could see the Rowan sapling that he planted the day before and wondered how big it would be when he would see it again.

Chapter 16

Tommy sat with his crew in the briefing room as the colonel explained their mission to them. His mind kept wandering back to Rachel. He wondered if she was sleeping or cleaning the house again. Possibly even replanting the seedling he planted for her... he chuckled quietly to himself.

"Lieutenant Smith? Lieutenant Smith!" the colonel's voice boomed.

Alex, his best friend and navigator on *Fifinella*, punched Tommy on the knee with his fist.

"Sir, yes, sir?"

"Did you hear that? You're going to be the lead plane... You up for that today, Lieutenant?" The colonel stood there with crossed arms, staring at Tommy.

"Sir, yes, sir."

"Good to hear. You better pay attention, Smith, and get up to speed. The other two planes are being flown by two rookie crews so show them the ropes up there."

"Yes sir. I understand our mission and its gravity. I'm ready to fly and drop our payload on the bridge in France-"

"Then you *were* listening." The colonel interrupted him before he could say more.

⋅⊰≡◉ਃ⋅

Before he knew it, Tommy was sitting in the cockpit and looking out the window of his B-17. As a simple farm boy, he'd never dreamt of flying a plane that would take up half a football field. His plane, the *Fifinella*, sat in an English countryside as its crew prepped for their next mission.

How perfect life would be if there wasn't a war. I could fly FiFi, delivering packages to Paris, and then go home to Rachel Smythe—I mean Smith.

He wondered if he would ever see her smile again, hear her voice, or listen to her laugh. He longed for the gentle touch of her hand, the kisses she gave him for no reason at all, the scent of her skin.

The crew began its normal complaining about the heat, the wait, when finally Tommy spoke up.

"Stop your bellyaching," Tommy interrupted. "Let's just get focused. How does *FiFi* look?"

Charles, his top gunner and flight engineer replied, "Shipshape and ready to roll, Cap."

For the next two hours they waited for the call to fly, almost figuring that their mission was cancelled. It was hot as hell inside *FiFi* and tempers flared.

All Tommy could think of was Rachel waking up alone in her bed, the fluffy comforter surrounding her as she lay naked. He pictured her pink nipples on her perky, soft breasts and how he would gently squeeze them, causing her to moan with delight. He could feel himself becoming aroused at the mere thought of her.

"... I told you, Calvin, you eat too damned much! All you think about is food!" Del, the radio operator, argued with the belly turret gunner.

"Whoa! Wait." He was quiet for a moment. "Let her roll, sir." Del said cutting into Tommy's fantasy. "We're clear to go."

Tommy cleared his throat. "Ladies, please buckle your seatbelts and keep your hands and feet inside at all times. Snacks and coffee will be served when we reach fifteen thousand feet. Enjoy the flight."

He taxied *FiFi* out to the runway. Locking the brakes as he revved the engines one more time, he double-checked the generator, locked the tailwheel in place, and set the gyros.

Tommy ramped up the engines and released the brakes, causing the plane to surge down the runway. *FiFi's* engines whined as he lifted the fifty-five thousand pound aircraft into the sky.

Ten minutes later, they could all see the English Channel down below. The sweltering ground heat that previously filled the cabin was replaced with cool, clean air.

"Listen up, guys, let's not fall asleep," Tommy said. "I know we all had fun last night and we all want to go home. It's not a training mission, so be on your toes. We don't want any surprises today, okay? I have a pretty little lady I plan on returning to. Del, put on some music."

"Yes, sir."

Harry James played through the speakers.

I'll get by / as long as I have you. / Though there may be rain / and darkness too, / I won't complain, / I'll see it through. / Poverty / may come to me, that's true, / But what care I? / I'll get by / as long as I have you.

Soaring through the blue sky for the next hour, Tommy's thoughts continued. *Rachel didn't want me to go. She said she had an uneasy feeling. But who doesn't? And damn those tarot cards. Yet look at this: no clouds, no antiaircraft fire, no German planes. What could possibly go wrong?*

I'm so close. I just need to finish five more missions and I get to spend the rest of my life with that beautiful, hot English girl who stole my heart. Tommy slipped his hand into his flight jacket, rubbing his fingers over the bruise she left when she bit his nipple.

"Cap," Alex said, "we're ten minutes from target."

"How's she looking, Ray?"

"Good, sir."

"Hey, Chuck, those guys falling into single formation?"

"Yes, sir."

"Ray, whenever you want, *FiFi's* yours. Be gentle with her."

"I'll take her now, Cap."

"Okay, Ray. Wake me when you're finished."

⊶⊜⊷

Rachel woke up suddenly in her bed feeling completely alone. She stayed there for a few minutes thinking of the last couple of days with Tommy. Before she got out of bed she heard the back door in the kitchen open. She hopped out of bed grabbing her robe—hoping it was Tommy surprising her because his mission had been scrubbed.

Rounding the corner and going into the kitchen she saw her best friend. "Oh, bloody hell, Izzy! I thought you might be Tommy."

"Well good morning to you, too. Would you like some tea? And close your robe, you hussy!" Izzy started a kettle of water to boil for tea. She rummaged around the countertop and found the cookies that Rachel made the day before.

Rachel stood looking out the window wondering if his mission had ended.

Izzy bit into the cookie. "Oh my goodness, these *are* Aunt Marilyn's cookies, aren't they?" She licked her lips and took another bite. "Mmmm."

"No! *I* made them." She smelled Tommy's cologne on her pink robe as she buried her nose into one arm of the robe.

"These? No way. They're too perfect."

"What are you saying?"

Between chews, Izzy said, "I'm saying that if Tommy were here, that would mean that I would be in bed with Alex. So sorry to disappoint you, it's just me, enjoying your cookies."

Rachel rolled her eyes at her best friend.

"I still think Aunt Marilyn made them."

"Give me a break, sis. I'm on edge and teetering, so don't push me. Besides, I don't feel that well at the moment." It hit her in the stomach and heart at the same time.

Izzy looked at Rachel. "Did you get *any* sleep last night?"

"Just a few hours here and there. Tommy and I spent a lot of time... oh, Lord! I feel like I'm going to-"

"You look a little green-" Izzy didn't complete the sentence.

At that moment, Rachel lurched for the kitchen sink and reached it just in time to vomit violently. Izzy jumped out of the way.

"Dear God! You're pregnant, aren't you?" Izzy asked in shock as she grabbed a towel.

⊶═◉◉═⊷

Tommy adjusted his body to a comfortable position in the pilot's seat. A loud explosion shook *FiFi*. Suddenly, the cockpit erupted into smoke and fire, with every alarm blaring. Tommy couldn't breathe from the burning smoke filling the cockpit.

"Bombs away!" Chuck shouted.

"Chuck!" Ray yelled out. Chuck grabbed a fire extinguisher as Tommy banked to the left to get out of the way of the other planes making their bombing run.

Stinging blisters formed on his right hand from the heat of the flames. His jacket smoldered as he brought *FiFi* down to ten thousand feet so the crew could breathe.

"Engine two shutting down, sir!" Louis screamed. "The hydraulic oil has caught fire and the oxygen exploded, Cap."

"Crew, report in!" Tommy yelled. One by one, he heard their names. Tommy looked at Louis and rang the bell three times–the signal to bail out. Then, as Tommy leveled out the plane at eight thousand feet, he gave one final, long ring.

"Go boys! I'm going to hold her steady!"

He whispered to *FiFi*, "Come on girl, I'm not leaving you. Not 'til the boys get off. Just a bit more, baby." Engine three began to smoke while he fought for control. Tommy banked around to distance *FiFi* away from the town below.

All the crewmembers jumped out when he heard the next explosion, followed by Alex screaming, "Cap, we need to go!" Tommy felt Alex's hand on his shoulder as *FiFi* started to tremble.

"You got to go, Alex!"

"Tommy, we'll find a way to land her!"

"Not without losing our lives. And that village below! Tell Rachel that I love her, Alex. Will you do that for me? Promise me!"

"I'm not leaving you!"

"Alex, this is not your ride. Go! Tell my sweet Rachel that I'm so sorry and that I love her like I've never loved anyone in my life. Tell her that I'll be back for her, the next time around."

Alex screamed something before he jumped, but Tommy couldn't hear anything anymore...

Like We Always Do

A Note from Ray and Deb

To our wonderful readers,

In 2012, Ray visited France to see his son's art exhibit. He scoured the Internet searching for different places to see during his stay. In the course of his research, he stumbled upon a picture of a woman in Incarville, France, standing next to a memorial for First Lieutenant Thomas P. Smith, a B-17 pilot killed in action on August 13th, 1944 in WWII. The memorial had an inscription describing how he sacrificed his life to save his crew and a small village.

Ray and Deb felt an otherworldly pull to Thomas P. Smith. Something nearly screamed at them that a story needed to be written about this brave hero who died on his plane, the *Fifinella*.

Does it matter whether it is fact or fiction?

We hope you enjoyed *A Lost Romance Found*. If you fell in love with Tommy and Rachel's love story, we hope you will read *Twisted in Time*, book one in *A Twisted Series*. Be on the lookout for our next book, *A Twisted Reality*.

The series is written about true love and how it can transcend anything–even lifetimes. Find out how the love story concludes, or continues...

Thank you.
Life Only Has Beginnings,
Ray and Deb

Visit MysticScribblers.com for updates and interesting past life information. Have you had past lives? Find out. Take the past life questionnaire.

If you enjoyed this book, help others find it so they can enjoy it too.

- **Recommend it:** Please help other readers find this book by recommending it to friends, readers' groups, and discussion boards.

- **Review it:** Let other potential readers know what you liked about this book.

Printed in Great Britain
by Amazon

80527584R00099